About the Author

After a globe-trotting adventure spanning six years, Simone has found her serene haven amidst Suurbraak's majestic mountains. Nestled in a charming cabin, solace awaits Simone alongside her partner Jaco and their fury confidants, Toffee, Wilson, Mona and Patat. Balancing her small business and writing endeavors, From cringeworthy poetry penned at the tender age of nine (hopefully, her mom burned those books), her enduring passion for all things artistic has never waned.

It's Okay

Simone Terblanche

It's Okay

Olympia Publishers
London

www.olympiapublishers.com
OLYMPIA PAPERBACK EDITION

Copyright © Simone Terblanche 2024

The right of Simone Terblanche to be identified as author of
this work has been asserted in accordance with sections 77 and 78 of
the Copyright, Designs and Patents Act 1988.

All Rights Reserved

No reproduction, copy or transmission of this publication
may be made without written permission.
No paragraph of this publication may be reproduced,
copied or transmitted save with the written permission of the publisher,
or in accordance with the provisions
of the Copyright Act 1956 (as amended).

Any person who commits any unauthorized act in relation to
this publication may be liable to criminal
prosecution and civil claims for damage.

A CIP catalog record for this title is
available from the British Library.

ISBN: 978-1-80439-926-2

This is a work of fiction.
Names, characters, places and incidents originate from the writer's
imagination. Any resemblance to actual persons, living or dead, is
purely coincidental.

First Published in 2024

Olympia Publishers
Tallis House
2 Tallis Street
London
EC4Y 0AB

Printed in Great Britain

Dedication

For Mom and Kiki
Love you

Jaco, for lifesies.

Acknowledgments

To all those who have become my cherished family throughout these years, I hold within my heart an immense love for each and every one of you.

Author's Note

It is important to recognize that abusive, jealous, and possessive behaviors should never be romanticized or glorified but rather taken as a warning sign. Although we all deserve a love that is worth writing books and poems about, it's crucial to remember that being alone is also a valid and safe option, regardless of age, gender, or family opinions. It's okay to prioritize your own well-being above all else, no matter the circumstances. To the strong female lead, I hope that something positive comes your way.

1

Demotivated.

A feeling of demotivation has taken hold of me. I let out a deep sigh and absentmindedly tug at my bottom lip with my pointer finger and thumb, my eyes fix on the unyielding text cursor that seems to mock me with each flicker. I reluctantly close my laptop and fold my arms, determine to identify the root cause of my lack of motivation and tackle it head-on. But what does 'demotivated' really mean? I wonder aloud before reaching for my phone with a hint of frustration, tapping out the words 'demotivation definition' in the search bar with a series of clicking sounds.

I am frustrated beyond belief. I have a looming deadline, yet here I am, wasting time on googling obvious definitions. Admittedly, my current life events don't quite align with the lofty standards I set for myself as a naive teenager with questionable influences. According to my overly ambitious plans, I should have been a famous author by now, happily married to the man of my dreams, and maybe even expecting a child.

Instead, I find myself swiping left and right on Tinder, Bumble, and Hinge, being bombard with unsolicitous dick pics and awkward small talk with the occasional *nice guy*.

I am twenty-six.

My clock is ticking.

My writing career has only just begun with the publication of one book, a poignant story inspired by my dear friend Zoe's own experiences. I added my own creative flair to her tale of love gone awry, resulting in a beautifully tragic story that resonated with readers.

I take pride in crafting stories that are raw, authentic, and relatable.

After my first book was published, a major publishing house took notice and offered me a contract, catapulting me into the ranks of published authors in America. However, now the pressure is on to deliver more books, specifically ones with happy endings. I struggle with this expectation as I prefer to delve into the complexities of relationships, even if it means exposing the heartbreak and pain that love can bring. But as the saying goes, 'love and sex sells,' and I must consider the demands of the market if I want to continue my career as an author.

As I sit here, desperately trying to conjure up more love stories to avoid being just another 'one-hit wonder,' my mind wanders aimlessly. I glance down at my half-drunk cup of cold coffee, wishing it could offer me some inspiration. Reality hits hard as I realize I need to leave soon for my day job, the one that pays the bills and puts food on the table. I let out a heavy sigh, feeling the weight of the pressure to deliver another successful book weighing down on me.

"Excuse me, can I get the check, please?" I ask the waitress, forcing a smile. As she nods and walks away, I lean back in my chair, feeling exhausted and, demotivated.

It's hard not to be hard on myself when I have so much to accomplish, but at the same time, it's difficult to find the energy to work or study. The truth is, as much as I love the idea of love and romance, I've never really experienced it in the way that books and movies portray it. There were no slow-motion montages or beautiful music playing when I lost my virginity – it was awkward and uncomfortable, and I kept my bra on the entire ten minutes.

On top of all that, society seems to constantly remind me that

I need to find a man to take care of me because, apparently, being alone at my age is unacceptable. And don't even get me started on the whole ticking clock thing and pressure to have children.

But do I even want children?

I'm not sure.

It's all just so overwhelming.

As a child, I was captivated by the grandiose tales of great love and the passionate pursuits of lovers in books and movies. However, in reality, the boys around me were far from the charming protagonists I had envisioned. Growing up, I was forced to witness the harsh realities of *love*, such as my father's dismissive attitude toward my mother when she tried to have serious conversations about their crippling marriage. Day in and day out, I watched my mother tirelessly attend to all the cooking, cleaning, and laundry while my father did nothing but make a mess.

And then, one day, I watched him go, leaving behind the bitter aftertaste of abandonment.

During my teenage years, I realized, yet again, that the boys around me were nothing like the charming and respectful teenagers I saw in the movies. Instead of holding open doors or shyly asking us out on dates, they made inappropriate remarks, objectified us, and bullied us when we fought back. It was a harsh reality that shattered my naive expectations of love and relationships.

No longer was I living in a romantic comedy with a perfect soundtrack and a handsome leading man.

It was a far cry from the truth.

I must admit, I did have one actual 'boyfriend' during my school years who stood out from the rest: Luke Davis. It's funny how vividly I remember him, even though our relationship mainly consisted of him waiting for me every morning for four weeks before school just to give me a super awkward, kind of painful one-armed hug while discreetly eyeing all the boys walking past us as if to signal to them that we were an *item*. Then, he would quickly run away, overcome with shyness. Despite the brevity and awkwardness of our 'romance.' I cherish those memories and the innocent sweetness of it all.

Unfortunately, Luke and I were unable to make things work at the tender age of ten. Juggling a healthy relationship and a successful school career proved too challenging for me at that time. I ended things with him behind the school bleachers after the fourth period. With newfound freedom as a single girl, I planned to enjoy my snack pack alone during recess.

Moving on to my college years, I encountered many boys who claimed to like me but were not willing to commit. Instead of settling, I chose to *date* those who I found attractive and wrote poetry about the man I truly desired. I became my own emotional support system, allowing myself to indulge in the fantasy of finding a partner who truly valued and appreciated me. I became completely consumed by my studies, dedicating all my time and energy to excel academically. In the little free time I had left, I took on extra shifts at the coffee shop where I worked. My determination to achieve top grades and secure financial stability motivated me to work tirelessly toward my goals. I was so focused on my aspirations that I would have worn my graduation gown onto the plane, if necessary, to leave this place as soon as I received my degree.

Fortunately, I was able to publish my book in my final year, providing me with the financial means to relocate to a small town, Shere.

A village in the Guildford district of Surrey. It had always been my dream to live in a quaint town with old-fashioned dial-up internet, a cozy fireplace, and within walking distance to any store.

Comfort, no hustle or bustle.

No fancy events or fuss.

Just me, my books, and a small town.

It was my own version of the 'Secret Window,' minus the murder and corn. Although Shere boasts a population that is not exactly what you'd call a small town. And with my high-speed, uncapped Wi-Fi, I'm not exactly living like the Amish.

And yes, I'm not that far away from the London *hustle and bustle.*

Regardless, I'm content here – this place is peaceful, and it feels like home. Plus, I landed a decent job at the Daily Shere, writing about the exciting events happening in town, from the Shere parade to cook-offs and even the great antique sales. It may not be the most thrilling content, but it's a great way to stay in touch with the community and earn a living. Most importantly, it leaves me with enough free time to pursue my true passion – writing my own books.

Leaving the coffee shop behind, I stroll down the road to the local bookstore, where I am covering a book signing event. Luckily, the shop is just a stone's throw away from the coffee shop.

These gatherings are typically relaxing affairs – a few local authors signing their books and a group of ladies selling homemade baked goods. I always find myself drawn to this lovely old lady named Barbara. Although her pastries are to die for, it is the way she makes me feel like one of her own granddaughters that kept me coming back.

It is comforting to have that sense of familial connection every now and then.

I wonder if Barbara knew that her name meant 'protectress of fire and lightning' in the Catholic sense (not that I am Catholic myself).

I enter the quaint bookstore and greet Barbara, the protectress of fire and lightning and the creator of scrumptious cupcakes. Her snow-white hair is neatly tied back with an orange headband, and her glasses perch on the tip of her nose. As she arranges the last of her cupcake boxes on the table, I rummage through my bag for some cash.

"Hi, Barb. How are you doing?" I ask, offering her a warm smile.

"Dakota, darling, I'm thrilled about today's festivities, and how are you?" she replies with a broad grin, handing me a delectable cupcake in a little box.

"I can't complain," I quip, handing over the money.

"That means you're staying out of trouble," she retorts playfully.

"I suppose I am," I say with a chuckle.

"Speaking of trouble, have you met anyone interesting yet?"

"I'm afraid not," I confess.

"Well, that's no fun. A young lady like yourself needs a companion," she remarks.

"That reminds me, my grandson is in town. He's around your age, and he's single, too. I'd love for you two to meet."

Grateful for the cupcake, I smile and take the box from her hands.

Did the fates conspire to bring me a romantic savior in the form of Barbara's grandson in response to my silent plea for love and companionship while at the coffee shop?

I doubt it.

As the man calls for attention over the microphone, the room falls silent, and I exchange another smile and nod with Barbara before making my way to a seat on the other side of the room. The speeches are given, and guests excitedly move around to purchase cupcakes and have their books signed by the local authors. I take notes and savor the delectable cupcake, relishing the serene atmosphere of the event. Although my work for the small article on page six is done by the end of the speeches, I remain until the very end, soaking in the ambiance and observing the attendees as they trickle out, leaving behind a peaceful room with only the owner, the cleaning crew, and Barbara. Something about being surrounded by stories and strangers puts me at ease, and I cherish these quiet moments.

As the night winds down almost completely, I grab my coat and approach the romance bookcase, perusing the titles as I nibble on my lip.

I realize what I need to do to make my dream a reality: write a sappy, cliché love story featuring a clumsy female protagonist who trips or bumps into the male lead so he can catch her.

I cringe at the thought, but I know it's what the bookshelves demand.

As I gather my belongings, I hear the front door open and close, but I'm too distracted by my phone to pay much attention. Suddenly, a gentle touch on my shoulder makes me look up to see Barbara and a strikingly handsome man standing next to her.

"Dakota, this is Harry, my grandson," she introduces with a warm smile.

I quickly slip my phone back into my pocket and stand up to greet him, feeling a slight flutter in my stomach. "Nice to meet you, Harry," I say, trying to keep my voice steady.

He extends his hand, which I shake firmly. "Likewise, Dakota. Barb has told me all about you," he replies with a charming grin.

I feel my cheeks heat up as I glance over at Barbara, who's beaming with pride. "She has, has she?" I ask with a hint of teasing in my tone.

Harry chuckles, his bright green eyes sparkling in the dim light. "Oh, don't worry, it was all good things," he reassures me.

I can't help but smile back at him, feeling a sudden surge of hope that maybe, just maybe, the gods of love and romance had heard my internal cry for help after all.

2

Barbara's eyes sparkle mischievously as she claps her hands together in excitement. "Why don't we continue the night with a cup of tea? It'll be so much fun!" Her eagerness is infectious, but I can see the not-so-subtle intention behind her words.

Harry chuckles at her enthusiasm before clearing his throat. "It's late, Nan. We can catch up another time."

"Nonsense! The night is still young. And I'm speaking from experience." Barbara retorts with a wink in my direction.

I can't help but smile at her playful nature, and Harry seems to be enjoying it, too.

"All right then," Harry relents, turning to me with a smile. "Would you like to grab a tea with me and my energetic grandmother here?"

"I'd love to," I reply, feeling a flutter of excitement in my stomach.

As we make our way to the door, Barbara stops us with a sly smile.

"Oh, you know what? I have too much to do here. You two, go ahead and have fun. I'll join you next time."

Barbara's not-so-subtle matchmaking attempts make me chuckle as we bid her goodbye and step out onto the street. Harry seems to find it amusing as well, as he chuckles beside me. We start walking toward the lively coffee shops ahead of us, the night air crisp and cool on our faces.

Harry tucks his hands in his pockets as we approach the coffee shop.

"So, are you just visiting?" he asks, his ears picking up on my accent.

"Ah, I've been living here for the past eight years, and yet, my American still shows," I joke, earning a chuckle from him.

"Eight years? How have I never seen you?"

"Probably because I prefer the comfort of my own home most nights."

Harry holds the door open for me. We enter the cozy shop and settle into a little booth in the corner, close to the heater. A friendly waitress in her mid-forties approaches us.

"Harry! Is that really you? You've grown so much since I last saw you!" she exclaims, embracing him with a kiss on the cheek and a warm hug. After a brief catch-up, she finally turns to me.

"And you! It's so great to see you out and about with someone! What can I get you kids?"

We both order hot chocolates, and the waitress disappears into the back.

"So, where in America are you from?" Harry asks.

"Los Angeles," I reply.

"And you decided that Shere was a better fit?" Harry prods.

"Way better," I affirm.

"May I ask why?"

I gaze into his light green eyes, feeling somewhat of a connection as if he understands, dare I say, me.

"To be honest," I begin, "I've always dreamt of living in a small town like this, where I can curl up by the fireplace with a good book and take peaceful walks. It may sound strange, but knowing most of the people in town, being greeted with warm smiles, and asked about my day feels amazing. Here, life isn't so rushed, and I have the luxury of time to reflect and think about what I want to write. I can jot down ideas while strolling through town, which is something I couldn't do in Los Angeles." As I pause, I realize I've been rambling, and I let out a little chuckle.

"It makes complete sense why you wanted to move," Harry says reassuringly. "So, you're a writer?"

I nod and smile. "Mmm hmm, I am."

Our drinks arrive, and they look delicious. After thanking the waitress, we're alone again.

Harry looks back at me, his gaze intrigue. "Tell me more about your writing. What kinds of books do you write?"

"I prefer writing realistic books if that makes sense," I reply. "I do love romance, but I like to write things people can relate to."

"So no Romeo and Juliet, huh?" Harry chuckles, taking a sip of his hot chocolate.

"You mean the story about the thirteen-year-old and the seventeen-year-old's three-day *relationship* that led to a total of six people dying, including a suicide?" I retort, making him choke on his drink.

"If you put it like that…" he concedes. "Do you have any books published?"

"Yes, in the States. It's a story about a girl who fell in love with a guy in the wrong place and at the wrong time. No happy ending." I take a marshmallow off the cream and pop it into my mouth.

"Of course. Does he die?" Harry asks, taking a bite of the cupcake Barbara gave us, licking his lips.

"No, no one dies; they just end up going their separate ways," I explain.

"Separate ways? With no more contact at all? I'm assuming someone was in love, right?"

"Yeah. She was," I confirm.

"And the guy?" Harry frowns as if he's seriously offended that they didn't end up together, but I smile at how invested he is in my story.

"Well, buy the book and find out," I tease, leaning back in my chair and tapping my fingers against the ceramic mug.

"Only if you sign it," Harry replies with a grin. With a warm smile, I take another sip of my hot chocolate before sharing the details of my book.

"The guy," I pause and bite my lip as I search for the right words, "he just vanished into thin air. No calls, no messages, nothing. It was like he never existed in her life, leaving behind only a bittersweet memory. Although he was the wrong guy for her, the book has its beautiful moments. You get to read about how much they enjoyed each other," I lean forward as I explain, using my hands as I talk, "You see, on paper, they had all the right ingredients for a healthy and lasting relationship that would make you believe that they were meant to be. But in reality, they lacked the important aspects of a relationship, like communication being the main one. So, she made a promise to herself that the next time she falls in love, she will make sure her love is cherished and reciprocated equally in a safe haven. Now, she's fully aware of her relationship standards. I hope my book will show people that everyone deserves something good, even after a heartbreak," I conclude with a small smile and a press of my lips together. "Or something like that."

He chuckles in response. "You're right; that's both beautiful and tragic. Writing out of experience?" He raises his eyebrows, curious.

"No, no, it did not happen to me," I clarify, continuing our conversation. "It kind of happened to my best friend, Zoe. I just added my own twist to it." As I sit back in my chair, grateful for the company of an inquisitive individual. "But, tell me, what do you do for a living?"

"I'm a business and building developer," he responds, and I can't help but be impressed by his very *mature* profession.

"Wow, that's like a real adult job," I joke, earning a laugh from him. "Was that what you wanted to be when you grow up?"

"I actually wanted to be an architect," he admits, his eyes lighting up at the thought. "I still design buildings in my free time, though."

"That's amazing," I say, truly impressed. "But, can't you do both professionally?"

He shakes his head. "Not really, there just isn't enough time." He smiles, and as we finish our conversation, he excuses himself to go to the restroom. I call the waitress over to ask for the bill, but to my surprise, she informs me that it's already taken care of.

"You're in the presence of a truly chivalrous gentleman," she says, squeezing my shoulder.

As Harry returns, he thanks the waitress again before placing his hand on my back, leading me toward the door. "You kids have fun!" she calls after us. "Please say hi to Barb for me, Harry, darling. And stay warm!"

I flash him a grateful smile, "Thank you for the drink," I say, fumbling with the buttons on my coat in an attempt to keep the cold out.

As he slips his hands into his pockets, Harry turns toward me with a hopeful glint in his eyes. "Hey, would you like to go for a walk?" he asks.

I nod eagerly, shivering a little but content for some company.

We walk up the street, our breaths misting in the cold air, until we finally reach the top of a hill overlooking the town. The sight before us is breathtaking: hundreds of little orange and white lights twinkling in the distance like fireflies on a summer night.

"I keep forgetting how big this place actually is," I say, shuffling around on the cold bench in search of a comfortable position.

"Yeah, me too," he replies, sitting beside me and gazing out at the spectacular view. His smile suggests he remembers something, and he brushes his fingers through his hair before chuckling. "This used to be my favorite spot in the whole town. My grandad would always bring me here after Barb fell asleep. She wasn't too thrilled about him taking a hyper kid to the top of a hill at night," he says, looking at me with soft eyes. "But after he passed away, I was so angry that he wasn't here any more that I forgot to appreciate the things that brought me closer to him, like this place." He smiles. His gaze drifting back to the view.

"It's cliché, but at the end of the day, it really is the little things that matter. We tend to forget how important they are, and talking about them is a great way to keep them alive when they're not around, you know?" I reply with a sigh. I catch him looking at me, and I smile in response. Our eyes lock for a moment before I break the silence.

"This view, it's like seeing everything from a whole new perspective," I say, admiring the stunning scenery before us. Harry nods in agreement before taking off his jacket and placing it around my shoulders. As I feel the warmth of the fabric, I can't help but notice the subtle scent of his cologne. We share a comfortable silence, lost in our own thoughts, as we gaze out at the twinkling lights in the distance.

I clear my throat and turn to him. "So, Harry..."

"Yes, Dakota?" He replies, his eyes meeting mine once more.

"What is the one thing you regret not doing in life?" I ask, resting my chin in the palm of my hand. Eagerly waiting for his response.

Harry lets out a laugh before answering, "Oh, this is an easy answer. Not getting my college band's name tattooed on my chest like I said I would."

I let out a gasp, pretending to be in shock. "Completely

unacceptable. Scared of needles?" I tease.

He shakes his head, still chuckling. "No, we broke up after a few weeks."

"Yeah, probably because you didn't get the tattoo," I joke, playfully nudging his arm.

Harry grins. "Oh, most definitely, I was the glue that held the band together. That and because of a girl."

"Naturally, did she not approve of the rockstar lifestyle?" I ask.

"You know, I think she enjoyed it more than we did, actually. Dated two bandmates at the same time." Harry chuckles, reminiscing on his mild rockstar days.

"Well, a girl has to keep her options open," I quip, earning a smile from Harry.

"True, but I will always blame her for taking away my opportunity to have 'not a king' tattooed on me."

I snort with laughter. "Oh, Harry, you need to call that girl and thank her.'

As Harry turns to me, his lips curl into a warm smile. "It's quite late and chilly. Can I walk you home?" he asks with a gentle tone.

I accept his offer gratefully, and as we descend the hill, his hand rests comfortingly on my back. The darkness envelops us, but soon enough, we approach the safety of the streetlights.

And finally, we reach my street and come to a stop.

I clear my throat, trying to calm my racing heart, and flash a smile as I attempt to tame my unruly hair; I unbutton his jacket, which I'm still wearing, and return it to him. "Thank you for letting me borrow this," I say appreciatively.

"You're very welcome," he replies, his hand brushing over mine. His eyes twinkle mischievously as he tilts his head and says, "Dakota, this may be forward, but I'd love to see you again."

I can't help but bite my thumb, hiding my giddy expression. "I would like that too," I confess, nodding.

Harry's smile widens, his dimples carving two charming indentations in his cheeks. "Okay," he says simply.

I chuckle, sweeping my hair behind my ear. "Would you like my number?" I ask, holding out my hand.

"Absolutely," he replies, placing his phone in my palm. I type in my digits, then hand his phone back to him. He takes my hand, and I feel a jolt of electricity course through me.

"Goodnight, Dakota," he says, his voice filling with warmth.

"Goodnight, Harry," I reply, my heart swelling with anticipation.

As our hands disconnect, he disappears into the night, leaving me breathless and excited for what the future holds.

3

With my piece on the Shere bookstore event now complete and sent off, I find myself with a bit of free time to tackle the mountain of paperwork before me. But as I stare blankly at the stack of documents, I can't help but wonder if they, too, will grow tired of our tedious relationship and simply disappear.

I grab the top sheet and begin to skim it, my eyes landing on a blurb about Prince Harry. I can't help but smile as I think back to last night, It was nothing short of amazing.

Who would have thought that Barb would have a grandson like Harry? He's incredibly charming, down-to-earth, and easy on the eyes. Our romantic stroll through the night, while he shared his thoughts on important matters, was enchanting. And when he gave me his jacket to keep me warm, I couldn't help but swoon, It was the epitome of romance.

My coworker Denise interrupts my reverie, poking her head out from behind her computer screen.

"What's got you grinning like the Cheshire cat?" she quips.

"Just thinking about lunch," I reply, trying to keep my thoughts to myself.

Denise is the mastermind behind the Dr. Q&Hey section of the Daily Shere, dishing out advice to individuals struggling to find love or navigate relationship problems. Her motto, 'It only starts with a hey, and the Qs will come after,' is catchy but slightly annoying when she insists on giving me unsolicited love advice.

While I have no doubt in her expertise, having found love

herself through the column, I can't handle the added pressure that comes with following her advice. The constant inquiries about my love life and the efficacy of her advice are enough to make me want to run in the opposite direction.

I don't want to come across as a buzzkill, so I politely decline any discussions about my love life at work. Instead, I simply smile and reply with a borrowed line from Denise's catchphrase, saying, 'I'm doing fine, just waiting for the right person to say 'Hey' to,' which Denise usually enjoys. She surprisingly hasn't pressed me for updates in a while. Of course, she does occasionally try to pry into my personal life, but I can handle that.

As I'm lost in thought, my phone buzzes on the table, and I glance down to see a text from Harry. A goofy grin spreads across my face, one that I didn't even know I was capable of.

"Is that lunch?" I look up to see Denise eyeing me with a smug look on her face.

"Yes, actually," I say with a wink as I turn my chair around to face away from her. Unlocking my phone, I read Harry's message:

Afternoon, Dakota.

I bite my lip and quickly type back, feeling giddy like a teenager texting her crush: **Afternoon, Harry.**

Another text arrives almost immediately, **So breaking the three-day text rule still gets you a reply. Guys everywhere will rejoice when word gets out.**

I can't help but chuckle at his comment.

Sometimes rules are meant to be broken, I respond.

I couldn't agree more. Any plans for lunch? He asks.

Yes, actually. I have a hot date with my desk and some peach yogurt, I joke.

Well, as lovely as that sounds, I'm not too far from your work if you care to join me for lunch? Harry suggests.

I'll meet you outside in a sec, I reply.

I grab my coat and make a beeline for the door, but Denise tries to stop me. "Where are you going?" she asks.

"Lunch," I smile as I hurry out the door.

As soon as I step outside, my heart skips a beat when I see Harry leaning against a mailbox, looking so effortlessly handsome. His face lights up when he sees me, and I take a deep breath as we walk toward each other.

"Hey," I say, looking up at him.

"Hey," he laughs, holding out his arm. "Ready?" I wrap my hand around his forearm, and we start walking down the street toward the little cafes. "So, hot date with your desk and peach yogurt, huh?" Harry jokes.

"I mean, sometimes it's mixed berries, depending on how adventurous I feel," I quip back.

We arrive at a cozy deli, and Harry graciously holds open the door for me, leading the way to a booth by the window. I can't help but smile as I glance out the window, observing the busy lunch crowd. Some people seem to be in such a rush that they barely have time to enjoy their meals, and the thought makes me frown.

Harry notices my sudden change in expression and gently asks, "You, okay?" I snap out of my thoughts and chuckle. "Yeah, sorry, just got lost in thought for a minute there."

As he hands me a cup of coffee, I explain my momentary lapse, "I was just thinking about how no matter where you are in the world, you're always rushing to work at some point."

Harry nods sympathetically and adds, "Ah yes, the nine-to-five that most people have and hate."

"That's so terrible, having a job you dislike," I comment. "I don't think I could survive a life like that."

Harry inquires about my own job, and I explain, "I mean, I wouldn't say I love it, but I like it. I get to write about people and all their things, which is nice."

He responds, "And I get to help people make all their ideas and dreams bigger and better, so that's pretty cool, too."

We share a smile as the waitress arrives with our food, and the aroma is divine. I bite my lip in anticipation and comment, "This looks so good. It reminds me of the burger John Travolta ate at that diner with Uma Thurman in Pulp Fiction. I was so hungry after that scene."

Harry admits that he's never seen the movie, and I excitedly suggest, "Well, I'm excited for you to see it. They're actually doing a Quentin Tarantino tribute this week at the Shere Theatre. I wonder if they'll show Pulp Fiction. We should go and see."

"We should," he agrees with a smile.

I playfully joke, "A woman asking out a man. Game changer. Women everywhere will rejoice when word gets out." Harry smirks in response.

As we finish our delicious meals, we stroll back to my office building. When we reach the entrance, we turn to face each other, and I play with my fingers as I look up at Harry.

"Thank you for lunch, Harry. It was definitely worth taking a break from my desk and yogurt."

"You're welcome, love. I had a great time."

"So, what day would you like to go to the theater?"

"How about tomorrow?" Harry suggests.

"Tomorrow works for me. The theater is actually just down the road from here, so I can meet you there if that's easier?"

"Why don't I meet you here, and we can walk together?" he proposes.

"Perfect. I finish work at four."

Harry leans in, and his seductive whisper sends shivers down my spine. "It's a date."

I inhale sharply as he gives me a gentle peck on the cheek before walking away. I climb the stairs to my office, my heart still fluttering from his innocent kiss.

Denise greets me with a smile.

"Lunch definitely agrees with you, D," she quips before returning to her computer screen.

The day of the long-awaited date has finally arrived. After enduring what felt like an eternity at work, I glance at myself in the mirror and give my hair a quick puff before heading downstairs to meet Harry. He's standing by the mailbox, engaging in a call, but upon seeing me, he gives a nod-smile and gestures towards the theater. As we begin walking, I notice a serious, firm tone in his voice as he talks about work; the conversation lasts for a few more seconds before finally hanging up.

"Sorry," he says, placing his phone in his pocket and running his fingers through his hair before smiling at me. "Hi."

"Hi," I chuckle, "Is everything okay?"

He nods, "Yeah," He looks at me intently, then shakes his head with a smile. "Let's not bore you to death before the movie. Don't want you falling asleep now."

"I'm not one to fall asleep during a movie, especially not a Quentin Tarantino movie," I smirk. "You can talk about work if you'd like."

Harry takes a step towards me and offers his arm, "I'd rather go see a movie with a pretty girl. Ready, Miss Dakota?"

The theater was only half full, as it is a mid-week screening. We sat at the back, right under the projector booth; a group of people walk in and take the front row. Harry and I exchange smiles as the lights dim; I struggle to focus on the movie's dialogue between bank robbers Honey Bunny and Pumpkin. Instead, I become increasingly aware of Harry's hand resting inches from mine. It was so close that a slight movement from me would make our fingers touch.

During the film, Butch exits Esmeralda Villalobos's cab and rushes upstairs to his apartment. Harry sat beside me, engross in the movie, but our hands remains still on the armrest. I glance down at them and wonder why I was hesitating. I could make the first move and just touch his hand. Even if it backfires, I can play it off as an accident. It shouldn't be such a big deal, and men don't always have to initiate physical contact.

We are both adults, and I scold myself for overthinking it, letting out a sigh.

Suddenly, Harry leans in, his warm breath tickling my neck as he whispers, "Bored?"

I smirk, shaking my head, and lock eyes with him. Our faces inch closer to each other, and I feel his skin brush against mine as our fingers intertwine. We are about to kiss, but Jules grabs Pumpkin, and Honey Bunny starts screaming, disrupting the moment. I jump in surprise, but Harry chuckles, and we settle back into our seats, still holding hands.

After the movie, Harry helps me with my coat and opens the door for me. As we walk toward his car, he places his hand on my back. I turn around to face him and ask, "And?"

Harry jokes, "You were right; that burger did look good."

We laugh, and I ask him how he liked the movie.

"Yeah, I really enjoyed it."

"Is that why you got distracted by my sigh?" I tease, and he chuckles, taking my hand, and we walk down the road, enjoying the cool breeze.

As we approach his car, Harry points to a sleek car in front of us. "This is my car," he says, unlocking the passenger door. "Roger the Royce. I inherited it from my grandad after he passed. It needs some fixing, but I love it." I ask him if it was from 1979, impressed by my semi-knowledge, he corrects me, saying it was a '76. I trace the top of the door with my finger. Harry takes my hand and suggests I drive. I eagerly accept the keys and dart to the driver's seat, adjusting it to my liking.

"I could get use to this," I say with a grin."

I turn off the engine and gaze at him, feeling a pang of sadness already creeping in. "You know, every time we have to part ways, I get this feeling that I don't want to. Are you some kind of witch?" He teases, hoping to lighten the mood.

"Well then, let's not say goodbye," I suggest.

"Oh? What do we say then?"

"How about 'see you later'? Or, if you want to be less cliche, we could always go with 'peace out'." I offer with a smirk, opening the car door.

Harry chuckles and steps out of the car; I lean on the roof of the car, arms stretched out, watching as he stands across from me with a look that's more serious than usual. His furrow brow gives him an air of mystery.

"Are you okay?" I ask, my frown mirroring his.

"You know, I wanted to wait." Harry's voice is soft as he steps closer to me, and I turn to face him, my heart pounding with anticipation. "Not rush things, you know. I mean, it's only been a couple of days." He steps up to me, his hand on my hip as he pushes me against the sleek curves of the car. I can feel the heat of his body so close to mine, and I can't help but bite my lip, caught up in the intensity of the moment.

He places a finger under my chin, lifting my face up to meet his gaze, his green eyes shining with an intensity that makes my heart skip a beat. "I wanted to do things right," he murmurs. "But we're all adults here." A mischievous grin curves his lips, and I can't help but smile in return.

He leans in closer, his body pressing against mine as he places both hands on my cheeks. Our noses are almost touching, and I can feel the heat of his breath against my skin. "If that's okay with you?" he asks softly, and I nod, feeling breathless and dizzy with desire.

Our lips meet in a kiss that's sweet and gentle at first, our mouths moving together in a dance that's as old as time. But soon, the pace picks up, and our tongues are tangling together in a passionate embrace that leaves me gasping for air.

My arms are around his neck as he presses his body even closer to mine, his hands moving down to my waist as he holds me tightly. I can feel the heat of his body against mine, and I never want this moment to end.

But eventually, we have to come up for air, and Harry rests his chin on my head as we catch our breath.

"Peace out," he whispers, and then he's gone, driving off into the night.

I'm left standing there, my heart racing and my mind reeling from the intensity of our kiss. Part of me wants to run after him, to beg him to stay, but the other part knows that this is just the beginning.

There will be other kisses and other moments.

4

As I gradually awaken on this gorgeous Saturday morning, the sun gently embraces my face with its warming rays. After a moment of blinking to adjust to the brightness, I stretch my arms above me and exhale blissfully.

As I reach for my phone, it stubbornly refuses to recognize my face, so I manually unlock it to discover a new message waiting for me:

Picnic by the hill at noon?

A smile spreads across my face as I eagerly respond, feeling a surge of excitement within me. **Sounds wonderful! Should I bring anything?**

The response comes quickly: **Just yourself.**

This newfound joy has ignited a spark in me, motivating me to finally start pursuing my publisher's dream and fueling my romantic creativity. It is inspired by a love story that's so romantic and cliche and soppy I feel it at the tips of my fingers, begging to be type out.

I would've scoffed at it just a few months ago.

But now, as I begin typing away on my laptop, it is beautiful in all its glory. I'm almost positive that my publisher will be smitten with it.

A gentle knock on my door interrupts my laptop-induce reverie, signaling that noon has arrived faster than expected. I was so lost in the pages of my new novel I only resurface to reality with the sound of knuckles rapping against wood.

"Hey," I greet my visitor, meeting his gaze as he extends his hand toward me. Without hesitation, I place mine in his, and he pulls me toward him, enfolding me in a warm embrace.

"Hey yourself," he replies, as my hands move on autopilot around him, caught up in the blissful bubble of just him and me. A sudden peck on my cheek brings me back down to earth, my feet finding their footing after a brief visit to the clouds.

"Ready?" he grins, his hands like two comforting hot water bottles on my waist. I nod, his hands gliding off my body, only to find my wrists as he playfully steps back, pulling me with him. He grabs the basket from my steps before turning toward the road, and we set off together.

After a brief stroll up the hill, we finally reach our destination. The myriad of lights that we marveled at a few nights prior are now still resting before their night shift. My companion spreads a cozy blanket on the ground and places the basket in the corner, beckoning me to join him with a gentle tap of his hand.

Taking in the fresh air, I sit down next to him, a smile on my face. He opens the basket, adroitly arranging the finger foods on the blanket before pouring us each a refreshing Mimosa.

Raising his glass with a sly grin, he proposes a toast, "To *our* spot."

I return his smile as our glasses clink together, our eyes lock in mutual adoration.

We take a sip, fully savoring the moment.

"Tell me about your family," I ask, cradling the glass with both hands.

"My dad, also Harry, is a cop, and my mom, Elizabeth, is a housewife."

"Oh, what did she do before?"

"She studied fashion, I think, or something related to clothing. But my dad wanted her to stay at home," he takes another sip before continuing, "and she loves it."

I can't help but feel a tinge of discomfort at the thought of a husband deciding his wife's career path.

And before I could catch myself, I voice my concern, "Did she have a choice?"

"Yeah, of course. She loves being at home," he says with a smile before leaning back to grab some grapes, offering me one.

Shaking off the uneasiness, I try to change the topic, but he beats me to it.

"How about you?"

I clear my throat before answering, "My dad left when I was younger; I don't know where he is. And my mom works a lot,"

Harry frowns, confused by my response, "Does she have her own business?"

I squeeze the grape between my fingers and say, "No, she has multiple jobs. Dad didn't just leave her; he left the bills too," I joke to ease the tension, "But she's happy, so it's okay."

Harry nods, trying to show me the sympathy in his eyes, "When was the last time you saw her?"

"Graduation," I say with a shrug.

His face drops, and he moves closer to me, tucking a strand of hair behind my ear, "I'm sorry."

I laugh, trying to lighten the mood, "It's okay. That's what FaceTime is for."

As Harry's intense gaze pierces through me, I wonder if he's doubting my words.

But I'm telling the truth; it *is* okay.

His hands snap me out of my thoughts as he pulls me onto his lap, and I laugh in surprise. He looks up at me with a smirk, "I think I would like some FaceTime now."

I roll my eyes at his cheesy joke before our lips meet, and I melt into his embrace. Our kiss is filled with passion, and I run my fingers through his hair, feeling his grip on me tighten. As we finally break free from the kiss, Harry's voice breaks the momentary silence.

"You, my dear, are going to be my date tomorrow." His hands still holding onto my body, my head presses against his.

"Okay." I breathe, and his grip on me relaxes as he sits back, using his hands as support. I open my eyes, feeling a bit dazed, like I just woke up from a dream. I look at him, his smirk telling me that his hold on me has reached a new level. It's like he has this weird power over me, turning me into putty in his hands.

I clear my throat, sliding off him and back onto the blanket, taking a big sip of my mimosa.

"May I ask where we're going tomorrow?"

"It's a work function," came the response, and I could feel my heart sink; the mere mention of a work function sends a wave of dread through me as I envision being trapped in a sea of unfamiliar faces, awkward small talk, and strained conversations.

The anxiety fills me quickly.

"Work function on a Sunday?" I couldn't help but express my dismay. Nevertheless, I try to mask my lack of enthusiasm with a forced grin. He nods, and I slump my shoulders, finally giving up the facade.

"Harry, I'm sorry, but I'd rather not go. I get a bit of anxiety at functions. And a work function sounds an awfully lot like you'll be preoccupied."

Amused by my reaction, he chuckles, "Don't worry, it won't be all business. You'll have a good time, I promise. Plus, you get to dress up."

The thought of dressing up didn't exactly excite me either, but I decided to play along and accept defeat. I give a weak smile, toying with the last few drops of liquid in my glass.

The next day, as we step into the hallway of an overpriced house, we're greeted by a butler holding a tray of champagne.

Everything looks expensive, surrounded by decorations that are probably only touched when being cleaned. Harry takes my hand and leads me onto the deck in the back, where we're greeted by more fancy faces dressed in suits and pretty dressed arm candy. I lift the side of my dress with my free hand, trying not to step on my own dress as I have in the last five minutes of being here. Harry hands me a glass of champagne as we walk towards a group of people with smiles plastered on their faces mid-conversation.

I break my gaze from the sea of sun-dresses and suits and look at Harry; he looks like he is in his element. I look back at the ocean of people in front of me.

So many sun-dresses and suits.

Harry warmly greets an older-looking man with a firm handshake.

"Ben, it's been too long," he says, eliciting a laugh from Ben as he pulls Harry into a friendly hug. Spotting a group of women by the snacks and drinks, Ben calls over to a brunette named Sian. She turns around and immediately flashes a smile upon seeing Harry. After giving him a hug and a cheek kiss, she extends her hand toward me. "And who is this?" Sian asks with a friendly tilt of her head. I introduce myself as Dakota, and we share a handshake. Ben steps forward to shake my hand, too, and remarks on my American accent.

"It's lovely to meet you both," I say, trying to hide my nerves. Sian and Ben banter with Harry, recalling the days when he was a mere recruit. Sian playfully slaps him on the chest before turning her attention to me.

"So, what do you do, Dakota?" she asks with a curious smile. Harry jumps in before I can respond.

"She's a writer," he announces before taking a sip of his drink. Sian and Ben are impressed, and I thank them with a smile.

As the conversation turns to business matters, I find myself nodding along without fully comprehending what they're talking about. Harry excuses himself, saying he'll be right back, and disappears toward a group of men. I'm left standing there feeling somewhat awkward, pretending to check my phone and scrolling through my photos. I look up to find Harry has vanished, and I decide to head to the bathroom.

After getting directions from a butler, I make my way down the hall and peek inside the library out of curiosity. The room is filled with vintage-looking books by renowned authors such as Bronte, Austen, and Dickens. I smile as I walk past the big wooden desk, dragging my finger over the spines of the books. I pull out Wuthering Heights and start to read chapter one, lost in the story, attempting to make my way to the desk. As I step forward, the hem of my dress snags on my heel again, forcing me to come to an abrupt halt as I struggle to free the tangle thread. Frustrated and off balance, I let out a groan mid-struggle. A voice laughs behind me, interrupting my annoyance. I look up to face the source of the interruption, still feeling awkward and unsteady.

The stranger, a dark-haired man, strolls towards me and kneels down to inspect my dress. His eyes meet mine briefly before settling on the snag. He gently takes my hand away, releasing the caught fabric, and then returns his attention to me with a charming smile. He rises slowly, perching himself on the edge of a wooden desk nearby, and quips, "Looks like I'm not the only one hiding from the party."

I nervously chuckle, feeling like a child caught in the act. "Thank you. And I'm sorry. I didn't mean to invade."

"You're not invading anything," he assures me. "What have you got there?" He gestures towards the book in my hands.

"Wuthering Heights," I smile, offering the book to him. He takes it gently, inspecting the cover before returning it back to me.

"Ah, good ol' Emily Bronte," he remarks, a smile still

playing on his lips. "A classic."

"A classic indeed," I agree, returning the book to its place on the shelf and leaning against the bookcase with my arms crossed.

The stranger narrows his eyes slightly, still grinning. "I'm Noah." He extends his hand for a shake.

I smile back and take his hand. "Dakota."

Noah gestures to my dress. "So, Dakota, did you come here to fix your dress, or do you always ditch business parties to hang out with deceased writers?"

"Well, deceased writers are much better company." I joke.

"I see. That's a shame," he replies, his eyes meeting mine again. "You seem like rather good company yourself, judging by your impeccable taste in my book collection." He winks, and I laugh.

"You might regret those words once you discover I'm feeling a bit Heathcliff–esque at the moment."

"In that case, I suppose it's worth mentioning that I happen to find Heathcliff rather intriguing."

Harry's throat clearing interrupts our conversation.

"Harry, always a pleasure." Noah smiles and stands up.

"I see you've had the pleasure of meeting my girlfriend," Harry remarks, his tone tings with a touch of arrogance, causing a slight discomfort to ripple through me. I lower my head, feeling a mixture of unease and disdain in response to his possessive tone. Sensing my reaction, Noah observes the situation and graces me with a warm smile.

"Yes, I suppose I have." His gaze back on me as he leans in. "It was lovely meeting you, *Heathcliff*." With a return smile, he walks past Harry and disappears into the hallway.

Harry approaches me, looking slightly annoying.

"Hey," I say, still leaning against the bookcase and watching him walk towards me.

"What was that?" he asks, his tone betraying his annoyance.

"I could ask you the same thing."

He pauses before grinning again. "Why are you hiding in here?"

"I'm not hiding," I reply, my arms still crossed. "I wanted to go freshen up, but I saw this and got curious."

"And Noah just happened to be here too?" he presses.

I furrow my brow, a hint of defensiveness creeping into my tone. "Harry, are you upset that I had a conversation with another man?"

He chuckles and reaches out to grasp my hands in his, pulling me closer until I'm standing between his legs as he perches on the edge of the desk with a sly grin. "Well, when I came back, I found my beautiful date missing, only to discover her laughing with another man; I couldn't help feeling a twinge of jealousy."

He winks and wraps me in a warm embrace, planting a tender kiss on the tip of my nose. "I just want you all to myself," he confesses, his eyes gleaming with affection.

"Okay," I say with a smile, allowing him to brush his lips against mine. "But next time, maybe don't disappear on me," I murmur the words against his mouth, and he pulls back slightly, his grip on me tightening. His smile remains sweet as he speaks, "I have to network and make sure I keep my job. You understand that, don't you?"

I nod, feeling uncertain about how to respond, but he doesn't give me much time to think before pressing his lips to mine in a quick, tender kiss before pulling away.

"We should head back before anyone starts wondering where I am," Harry suggests, rubbing my shoulders with a warm smile.

I nod, taking his hand as we make our way back to the patio where the other guests are mingling. But as we walk, my dress catches on my heel again, frustrating me to no end. "You go on ahead, I'll catch up," I tell Harry, gesturing toward the patio.

He nods and exits through the door, leaving me to deal with my wardrobe malfunction. I slump onto a nearby bench, feeling defeat and ready to go home. As I struggle to fix my dress, Noah appears before me, holding a pair of scissors in his hand. "We really have to stop meeting like this," he jokes as he kneels down to help me. "I saw you struggling and figured I'd help you get rid of the problem once and for all."

"Getting rid of the problem would mean burning this dress and tossing the shoes," I quip back, sitting back with a sigh.

"Let's go for the less dramatic option for now, shall we?" Noah chuckles, gently tugging the dress before cutting off the stubborn piece. "I take it this isn't really your scene?" he asks as he joins me on the bench.

I give him a small smile before answering honestly, "No, not really. I just really want to go home."

"Then why are you still here?" he asks, my eyes drifting toward Harry and the other guests.

He follows my gaze, and we catch Harry's eye. He glances at me and then at Noah before continuing his conversation with Ben. Noah notices, "Ah, I see. Well, if it's any consolation, this isn't really my thing either."

I laugh at his response, "Isn't this your house?"

"Yes, it is. But I'd rather be hanging out with deceased writers," he says with a grin. "They are much better company."

I smile, nod, and look back at the glass doors. As he gets up to leave, he places a reassuring hand on my shoulder. "See you around, Dakota," he says with a friendly squeeze.

I watch him walk away before bracing myself to join Harry outside.

As the party winds down, I'm relieved that it's finally over. I've exhausted my repertoire of fake smiles and nods, and I'm ready to call it a night. Harry has been fully immersed in conversation with the other guests, leaving me feeling bored and unengaged. As we say our goodbyes and are about to exit the party, I catch Noah's eye; he raises his drink in a friendly gesture before we disappear out of view.

5

A heavy silence hangs in the air as we make our way to my house.

It's hard to tell if Harry is simply tired or annoyed. I don't know him well enough to decode his moods yet.

As we pull up to my house, he shuts off the engine and turns to face me.

"Let me make it up to you," he says, taking my hand in his.

"Make what up to me?" I ask, caught off guard.

"Today," he replies, giving me a sweet smile. "I just want to make things right."

I hesitate, unsure of what to say.

"Nothing is *wrong*; today was fine," I lie, squeezing his hand.

Harry's lips press together, and he tilts his head slightly. "Fine enough that you preferred the company of another man instead of mine?"

I scrunch up my nose at his comment, but before I can respond, he continues. "I don't want to end tonight on a sour note. I just saw how uninterested you were. And I would like to make it up to you."

"Harry, I was not uninterested; you were busy the whole time we were there," I point out. "Am I not allowed to talk to other people?"

He narrows his eyes, quiet for a moment before he says, his voice softening. "I want to do something special with you. Let me walk you to your door, and we can plan something for tomorrow."

I agree, and as we walk to my front door, he takes my hand in his. "Tomorrow, after work, we can do whatever you want," he promises.

As we stand facing each other, Harry's eyes never leave mine, knowing he is waiting for me to answer.

"Hiking." I finally say.

"Jesus, this is one hell of a hike," he says, out of breath as we finally reach the top. We sit down on a rock, both of us panting, and take a swig of water. Despite the gloomy weather, the view was stunning, and the hike was just what *I* needed.

"You know, when I said 'anything you want,' I was thinking more of a fancy dinner or something," Harry jokes.

I smile. "Playing dress up is fun, but not always."

"You really don't like fancy, huh?"

"I don't mind it."

"Okay? So what was the problem yesterday?"

"I told you. Being surrounded by a lot of people, I don't know, forced small talk." I look toward the sky with a sigh, "Just gives me a bit of anxiety."

"Well, you might want to get used to it," he says with a grin. "I have to go to a lot of those." I inwardly groan at the thought, but Harry quickly adds, "But I'll take you on so many hikes to make up for it."

"Can't you hire a date?" I pretend that it's a joke, but I'm secretly hoping he says yes. He laughs at my fake smile, grabbing my hand so I am facing him.

"Now, why would I do that when I already have the prettiest one?"

I sigh as we start to make our way down the mountain. Harry asks, "Have you started on another book yet?"

I grin, feeling proud of myself. "Yes, I have, actually."

"That's good." He pauses, and we slowly make our descent,

"Are you going to quit your job at the Daily Shere?"

I shake my head. "Not anytime soon."

"Wouldn't it be better if you could stay at home and write more?" he asks.

I shrug. "Maybe, but I wouldn't have a solid income to pay the bills and buy food."

"What if I help you?" he offers.

I stop in my tracks, surprised. "Thank you, Harry, but no. I like making my own money."

He raises an eyebrow. "What if we have kids?"

I chuckle nervously as I start walking again, not wanting to have this conversation just yet. "Don't you think it's a bit early for that?"

"I'm just curious," he says, pulling my arm to stop me. "Would you keep working then, too?"

"Yes, I would."

"You would?"

"Yes. Okay," I hesitate, "This is definitely an important conversation that we absolutely should have, especially if we're going to keep seeing each other. Kids are great, but I'm not 100% sure right now that I want any. And if I do decide to bring another life into this world, then yes, I will go back to work. Women don't all want the same things, Harry." I admit, "We're not all housewives," Harry's face drops as soon as the words leave my mouth. I immediately regret saying it and try to backtrack. "Wait, I'm sorry, that came out wrong. I didn't mean it the way it sounded."

The silence between us was deafening as Harry let go of my arm and motion down the path. "Let's get going," he says curtly.

I curse myself for being so thoughtless as we get into the car. Harry was giving me the cold shoulder; I guess it may have sounded like a dig at his mother.

Did it, though?

I don't know.

"Harry, I really am sorry," I apologize, hoping to make amends. "I didn't mean to offend you or your mom."

"I just need to stop by my place quickly before I drive you home," Harry says before starting the car. I lean back in my seat, letting out a sigh as we drive off. I can't stop thinking about how to make things right. This shouldn't be so difficult; we are still in our honeymoon phase, or at least we are suppose to be.

We arrive at Harry's stunning white house, enveloped in lush gardens blooming with roses. As Harry parks the car, he surprises me by taking my hand and leading me up the steps to the main door. The dimly lit hallway, with black tiling, glass displays, and warm lights, takes my breath away. At the end of the room, big windows offer stunning views of London.

"Wow," I breathe out in awe. Harry laughs, breaking the spell of silence, and guides me to the kitchen, offering me a cup of tea with a smile. As I gaze out the window at the breathtaking view, I can't help but sigh, "I bet the stars look insane from up here."

Despite our earlier disagreement, Harry opens up about his love for astronomy, and I find myself completely mesmerized. As he talks about the stars and planets, his eyes light up, and I can't help but feel my heart flutter with admiration for him. Memories of stargazing with my mother flood my mind, and I share them with Harry. "No matter where we were in the world, my mom would always point out the Three Sisters to me. It became our little thing."

Harry gazes at me with such intensity that I feel my heart race in my chest. As he brushes a strand of hair behind my ear, our lips meet in a gentle, romantic kiss. The heat rises in my cheeks as I try to steady my breath, enjoying the moment.

"I should get you home," Harry says against my lips, and I nod, feeling a sense of disappointment that our kiss had to end.

I sink back into my seat, resting my head against the headrest, and take a long, leisurely look at him. I observe every inch of his face, completely engrossing in his features. With a lack of any substantial conversations to occupy my attention at the function, I found myself stealing glances at Harry throughout the day. I observe the subtle movements of his eyes, noting how they narrow with intense focus and crinkle ever so slightly when he chuckles. I couldn't help but study the curves of his lips, which seem to convey a multitude of emotions. When he was listening intently, they would be tightly pursed, but when he was sincere, they would stretch into a wide, dimpled grin. And when he made a joke, they would form into a playful, almost mischievous smile.

Suddenly, he catches my eye and grins, a sight that never fails to make my heart swell. His entire face lights up, imbuing a sense of safety. Even in the midst of a fire, everything would be all right as long as he smiles at me.

My thoughts drift to his dimples – those adorable quirks that make him all the more endearing. It's funny how a genetic defect that results from shortened facial muscles can bring me so much joy. My heart flutters every time his dimples appear, akin to the sensation of being on a rollercoaster at its peak, looking down at tiny ants below. Then the ride drops, making my heart skip a beat before finally coming to a stop. That's how I feel every time I see his smile, and I can't help but smile back in response.

Harry's voice breaks through my reverie, and I return to reality. "What's got you grinning like that?" he asks, squeezing my leg affectionately. I reply.

"I'm just looking at you." He winks, and I squeeze his hand

in response.

Harry walks me to my door; feeling like we seem back to our old selves again, I invite him in for a drink. After placing my bag down on the table, I turn to see Harry already looking at me, casually leaning against my kitchen counter.

"Come here," Harry beckons; I grin playfully but hesitate, feeling a little self-conscious after our hike.

"I'm pretty gross right now," I reply with a chuckle.

Harry's eyes twinkle with mischief as he approaches me, reaching out to tuck a loose strand of hair behind my ear.

"I'm sure I can handle it," he whispers, his voice low and sensual, sending shivers down my spine.

I laugh, feeling the tension between us building with each passing moment. Harry sits down on the chair behind him, pulling me in between his legs as our fingers intertwine. As our eyes lock, I scan his face, admiring his handsome features.

Harry looks fine again, with no trace of anger or upset.

He looks better.

His hands slide down my thighs, pulling me in for a kiss and onto his lap, sending shockwaves through my body as my legs dangle on the sides of him, my eyes flutter close as I feel his smile grow wider, his lips trailing kisses down my neck.

"I'm pretty gross too; perhaps we should go take a shower," he smirks into my neck, his grip on my thighs tightening as I nod absentmindedly, eyes still shut, feeling a tingle of anticipation course through my body as he lifts my chin and pulls me in for a soft, lingering kiss.

With a sense of urgency, he lifts me up, carrying me toward the bathroom.

Steam from my shower fills the air, and our bodies entwine in the enveloping fog.

We're wrapped in our cozy towels; I'm nestling between his legs, my head resting on his chest whilst my wet hair sticks to my neck, his fingers delicately caressing mine. The room is dark, allowing us to take in the breathtaking view of the stars shining through my window.

We're content in each other's company, cherishing the silence that speaks volumes. As we sit there, lost in our thoughts, I can't help but wonder if we could freeze this moment in time. His gentle touch and the peaceful ambiance of the night make me feel incredibly fortunate and elated. I let out a deep sigh, and Harry pauses his finger play, turning his head to check his watch and then focuses his attention on me. "The sun will be up soon. I should start heading home."

As he heads to the side of the room to gather his things, I sit up, hugging my legs. I watch the sky change from a deep blue to a purple hue and then gradually shift into a warm, reddish color. I'm exhausted, and although I was determined to stay awake, wanting to savor every moment with him, I need to rest.

I wander off to the bathroom to splash some cold water on my face. Looking at myself in the mirror, I can't help but notice how happy I look.

It's lovely having someone who makes me look so happy.

A now clothed Harry walks over to me and wraps his arms around me, lifting me off my feet and carrying me back to bed.

We collapse onto the bed, giggling as he peppers my face with kisses. "I'll text you later, yeah?"

6

As the days turns to weeks, I discover a profound sense of longing whenever we were apart, a deep homesickness that seemed to render me helpless in solitude. It was as if I had forgotten how to be alone, as all my free moments became completely consumed by Harry's presence. Yet, in those instances when we were reunited, everything fell into perfect alignment once again.

Hand in hand, we wandered through landscapes, cherishing each other's company. From sharing popcorn during movie nights to playful laughter as we walked back to the car, our connection felt effortless. Intimacy permeated our lives, whether it was in the bedroom, the shower, or the kitchen.

Harry seized every opportunity to be with me, disregarding any other commitments, which made writing my third book a real challenge.

However, the moment Harry appeared with a big bouquet of flowers, chocolates, or other thoughtful gifts, my writing was forgotten in an instant.

We were inseparable. It finally felt like I was living in my very own romantic comedy, and I was the star of the show.

Harry's voice startles me out of my trance as he declares, 'We're going on a fancy date,' with his head burried between my legs. I bolt upright, my eyes wide with surprise. 'What?' I gasp, wondering why he chose such an inopportune time to reveal his plans.

'Yes, tomorrow,' he confirms, his lips trailing kisses up the inside of my thigh and his hands clasping my waist. Instantly, I'm rendered speechless and deaf to everything else he's saying. After we finish, our breathing ragged, he turns to me with a smile. "Make sure you wear a dress that won't cause you any trouble this time," he jokes as he springs up and heads to the bathroom.

My anticipation for this date quickly sour into discomfort as I discover that Harry had actually brought me to his year-end work function. When I caught sight of Ben and Sian among the somewhat familiar crowd, my body went numb. I loosen my grip on Harry's hand, causing him to look at me quizzically. I struggle to maintain my composure—should I confront him now or try to hide my discomfort until the end of the night?

I wasn't sure.

He could've just told me that it was a function instead of letting me come in blindly.

He tugs at my hand, but I pull back slightly, searching his face. I spoke hesitantly, "I'm sorry, I just thought we were going on a date."

He lets out a sigh. "Dakota, I told you it was my year-end function."

I narrow my eyes, trying to remember when he had told me. His grip on my hand tightens. "We're here now, don't make a scene, okay?"

"I..." Before I could finish, he abruptly let go of my hand and walks away, leaving me feeling like complete crap. I had never caused a scene before, and my anxiety would never let me draw unwanted attention. So why did he assume that I would?

I need a drink.

I find an open seat at the bar, order a drink, and scan the room. Harry is chatting with a group of men while their wives stood beside them with tight-lipped smiles. The barista sets my drink down in front of me with a smile before disappearing back into the crowd of other baristas.

Don't make a scene repeats over and over in my head. Did I look like I was about to cause a scene? Harry hadn't even seen me upset, so how would he know? Maybe I had a strange expression on my face that gave him the wrong impression. Even though I knew that I would never cause a scene, it was possible that it could have looked that way.

"Heathcliff," a voice calls out, snapping me out of my internal turmoil. I look up to see Noah's smiling face, gesturing toward the empty seat beside me.

"Is this seat taken?"

"No, be my guest," I reply, managing a smile without forcing it. "It's nice to see a semi-familiar face," I add with a laugh as Noah settles in beside me.

"It is indeed. How are you doing?" he asks, his sincerity evident.

"I'm…" I begin to utter a response, but an unexpected wave of emotions wells up inside me, and tears threaten to spill over.

Oh god, why now?

Perhaps it's the sincerity in his voice that pierced through my defenses. It's been so long since someone asked me such a simple question with genuine intent. Conversations with Harry, on the other hand, rarely delve beneath the surface. Beyond the moments of intimacy, our discussions tend to be a string of silly sentences that hold an illusion of depth but lack any real substance.

So, how am I doing?

I'm confused, upset, and overwhelmed by the sudden realization that the foundation of Harry and I's relationship may be built solely on physicality, lacking true intimacy, closeness, and shared experiences; what we share is just superficial small talk sprinkled with meaningless gifts and sex.

Do I even know the real Harry?

Another realization hits me like a ton of bricks, and it's evident that Harry and I need to talk to truly communicate.

I take a sip of my drink, looking away from Noah. I force a smile after swallowing the alcohol in my mouth, "May I ask you something?"

"You may," he smiles as he scans my face, noting my quick change of the subject.

"Do you actually enjoy these events?" I inquire, gesturing around the venue. Noah chuckles, shifting in his seat as he observes the crowd.

"No," he responds with refreshing honesty, his gaze returning to meet mine. I find solace in his candor and offer a smile, nodding as I take another sip.

"Are you obligated to be here?" I inquire further.

"Obligated isn't quite the term my father would use," he remarks, glancing away momentarily and tapping his fingers on his glass. "But I am certainly expected to be present."

As I study his face, still gentle despite his serious expression, he meets my gaze once again, a faint smile playing on his lips. "My father owns this company, and that house was merely a gift among many, a form of bribery. He wants to ensure that the company remains within the family, using those gifts as leverage. It means I have no choice but to be here. It's all about appearances."

Taken aback by his openness, I can't help but fixate on his eyes, anticipation building within me.

There's a burning question on the tip of my tongue.

"What is it that you truly want to do?" I ask in a soft, hushed tone. His smile widens as my words reach his ears.

"You know, you might be the first person to ever ask me that," he chuckles, his gaze locks intently with mine. "I've always been drawn to the idea of writing books, but I quickly realized that I'm more of a reader than a writer." He jokes, and I find amusement in his response and laugh, prompting him to lean in closer, ensuring our conversation remains confidential. "But between you and me, I have a genuine passion for cooking. Owning a restaurant would have been my dream."

"Well, I happen to love eating food, so I probably would have been your most loyal customer," I retort playfully, a smirk on my lips. Noah's eyes never leave mine, his smile stretching from ear to ear as he slowly sits up straight once more.

"What about you?" he asks curiously. "What do you do?"

"I'm a writer, Noah," I reply with a small smile. His face lights up, shaking his head in apparent delight as he takes another sip of his drink.

"Why am I not surprised, Heathcliff?" he remarks with a wink. He glances behind me and then back at me, his expression curious. "Why are you sitting here all by yourself? Where's Harry?"

My heart sinks as the rush of emotions from earlier floods my senses, and Noah's perceptive eyes catch on to my turmoil. Before I can respond, he reaches out and gently places his hand on my shoulder, his voice fills with empathy. "Would you like to step outside for some fresh air?"

Caught in a moment of uncertainty, I hesitate, my mind grappling with the consequences of Harry witnessing me conversing with Noah again. I scan the room and glance over at Harry, still deep in conversation with a group of men, ignoring my presence entirely. Sensing my reluctance, Noah gives me an understanding smile. "Hey, we don't have to go if you're not comfortable."

After a brief moment of contemplation, I nod slowly.

"Actually, fresh air does sound nice."

As Noah and I stroll through the serene garden, the rustling of leaves and the chirping of crickets fill the silence between us. We soon find ourselves on a secluded bench under a canopy of trees, a perfect spot for introspection.

"I'm sorry, this is probably not the company you expected," I say, feeling guilty for burdening him with my emotional baggage.

"No need to apologize," Noah assures me with a gentle smile. "Sometimes, silence is the best company."

His words put me at ease, and I appreciate his understanding.

"But if I may," he adds, leaning closer to ensure I hear what he has to say, "you are welcome to say whatever is on your mind. I'm here to listen without any judgment."

His sincerity touches me, and I feel a sense of relief. Perhaps he can help me unravel the mystery of Harry's intentions, of what he really meant, and maybe even shed some light on my overwhelming realization. As I'm about to pour out my thoughts, my phone interrupts us with a ding.

I check my phone, half-expecting a message from Harry, but it's a notification from Zoe. The unexpected message causing me to frown.

"Everything okay?" Noah asks, concern etches on his face.

"It's my best friend Zoe. She's coming to London for two days," I share, a hint of excitement in my voice. "The ship she works on is docking in Southampton in a few weeks, and she wants to meet up."

"That's great. When was the last time you saw her?" Noah inquires, his interest genuine.

"Jeez, years ago," I reply, chuckling at the memory. As I recount some of the memories to Noah, he chuckles as he listens intently. I tell him about her job and the boy who broke her heart and how it's the reason for my first book. He nods along to my words as we laugh and share more and more stories.

Noah's next words catch me off guard, "It looks good on you."

"What does?" I ask, perplexing.

"Happiness," he replies with a grin; he looks at his watch and frowns. "We've been here for quite a while."

I sigh as I realize I should probably go back inside and find Harry. Noah stands up, extending his hand to me; I smile as I take his hand before he helps me to my feet.

I feel grateful for his kindness and support. I turn to him, feeling the need to express my gratitude.

"Noah?"

"Yes?" he turns to face me. I wrap my arms around him, hugging him tightly. He seems to understand as he responds, his arms enveloping me in a warm embrace.

"Thank you," I whisper, feeling a sense of comfort and belonging, grateful for this friendship.

As I make my way toward Harry and his group of friends, Sian greets me with a quick hug before Harry turns to face me. However, his reaction is far from welcoming, his shoulder turning cold against me. Sian leads me to the table and begins talking excitedly about Harry's new promotion, her eyes fix on mine as she takes my hands after I place my bag on the empty seat near the talking men.

"You must be so excited!"

"Excited?" I manage to utter, attempting to maintain a composed tone despite the overwhelming confusion surging within me.

Sian chuckles, her gaze shifting between Harry and me. "Oh, China will bring so much excitement, both for you and Harry," she exclaims as if it were the most obvious thing in the world.

"China?" I repeat, my voice feigning interest while desperately scanning Sian's face for any signs of deception.

With an air of enthusiasm, she continues, "Absolutely! It's been in the works for weeks. You and Harry are set to embark on a thrilling journey. Harry will be designing a remarkable building for a promising new business in Beijing. It's an incredible opportunity!"

My heart drops as I realize the reality of the situation. The thought of leaving everything I have here to travel to East Asia fills me with dread. I try to suppress my panic, reminding myself not to make a scene. I manage to maintain my smile and nod as Sian continues boasting about her time in China with Ben.

As the night unfolds, I maintain a composed exterior, but my mind is ablaze with a whirlwind of unanswered questions.

How long has he been aware of this promotion?

Why did he choose to keep it a secret?

Did he presume I would unquestioningly accompany him to China?

To simply abandon everything—my home, my job—and blindly follow him? This is exactly what I meant when I said we lack communication. Such a significant decision should have been thoroughly discussed beforehand.

How did I not notice this about him before? I feel like hurling something across the room, but Harry's voice kept echoing in my head, "Don't make a scene."

To top it all off, the fact that Harry is giving me the cold shoulder all night only adds to my frustration and confusion. It's like he's deliberately avoiding me or, worse, punishing me for something. His demeanor had turned even more icy since I returned from getting fresh air with Noah, and it's making me uneasy. As the night drags on, I continue to force nods and strained smiles until I reach my quota and reach for my bag to grab my phone.

But it's gone.

Panic sets in as I realize I might have left it on the bench outside.

Scanning the room for Harry, I spot him shaking hands with Ben. I make a move to go look for my phone, but Harry grabs my hand and pulls me toward the exit. I try to resist, but he ignores my protests and leads me to his car.

As he opens my door, Harry suddenly pulls me closer and kisses me roughly. I push him away, stunned and confused.

"What are you doing?" I ask, taken aback.

Taking a deep breath, Harry rubs his face before looking at me intently.

"Get in the car," he orders me firmly.

"I'm sorry, Harry, I really need to find my phone. I think I left it outside," I try to reason with him, my frustration evident in my voice.

But he's already in the driver's seat, his jaw clenches in determination as he starts the engine.

Defeated, I let out a sigh.

"It's all right. You can go. I'll find it," I offer, reaching out for my jacket on the passenger's seat. Before I can grab it, Harry smacks the steering wheel, causing me to jump.

I look up at him, and my heart sinks at the sight of his visibly upset expression. "I have your fucking phone, Dakota," he grits out through clenching teeth, still staring straight ahead. "Now get in the car."

Uncertain of what to do, I hesitate for a moment before relenting and getting into the car. My mind races with questions and confusion as we speed off into the night.

7

The car ride to Harry's house was tense; the silence in the air was palpable. Harry's knuckles were white as he held onto the steering wheel with an iron grip. My heart was pounding so hard that I fear he might hear it and get even more upset. When we screeched to a stop in his driveway, he slammed the car door shut and walked to his front door, stopping abruptly. I hesitantly get out of the car and follow him. As he closes the door behind us, the thick silence enveloped us, making me feel suffocated. Harry walks to the kitchen, pours himself a drink, and sighs heavily. I stand in the hallway, uncertain of what to do next. Harry takes my phone out of his jacket pocket, dropping it on the table.

"Your conversation with Zoe was interesting," he says, taking another sip of his drink without looking at me. My gaze shifts from my phone resting on the table to him, a bewildered expression etched on my face. I hadn't mentioned anything about Harry or Noah to Zoe.

What on earth was he talking about?

"What?" I ask, barely above a whisper.

"Don't play dumb, Dakota. I saw the messages," he retorts, his glass crashing down on the table as he abruptly turns to confront me. Snatching my phone from the table, he hurls it to the floor in front of me. "So, you're going to a bar."

"You went through my messages?" I ask, my voice quivers with a mix of violation and shock as I finally register that he had taken my phone from my bag and invaded my privacy by reading my messages, the weight of his actions sinking in.

His glare intensifies, and he bellows, his voice laced with anger, "First, you vanish for most of the night, doing God knows what with my boss's son, and now you want to behave like some slut in a bar? Why do you insist on humiliating me like this?"

I am taken aback by his words and feel insulted. I breathe, shaking my head in disbelief, taking a step back.

"Oh, I can't voice my feelings on something that bothers me, Dakota?" Harry retorts, his voice fills with anger.

"Harry, I'm just going to see Zoe." I point out, looking at my phone on the floor and then back at him. "When were you going to tell me about China?" I ask hesitantly, changing the topic. He frowns and looks away.

"I wanted to surprise you. I thought China would be a good place for us," he replies; shaking my head, I bend down to pick up my phone and see the new crack on the screen. Anger surges through me as I realize my hard-earned phone is now damaged for no good reason. Harry looks at me, inspecting my phone screen, before bending down and taking my hands in his, "I'll make sure to have your screen replaced," he says with a reassuring tone, placing his fingers under my jaw and lifting my face so I look at him. He brushes a piece of hair behind my ear and says, "I just care about you so much, Dakota. I can't stand the thought of you going anywhere dangerous. I worked so hard for this promotion and for our relationship, you know?"

"Harry," I say with a heavy sigh. "I'm sorry, but I can't go with you."

Harry's hand hovers near my face, but when he finally touches my neck, his jaw clenches.

"Let's talk about this first," he says, wrapping his fingers around the back of my neck.

"Okay. You should have told me earlier instead of assuming I would leave everything behind to follow you," I reply, trying to keep my voice steady.

"Dakota, please," he pleads, but his grip on my neck tightens. I take his hand from my neck, gently pulling it away as I slowly get up from the floor.

"How long have you known?" I ask, leaning against the kitchen counter. He doesn't answer and instead walks over to his drink on the counter behind me. "Is that why you asked me if I would quit my job?"

"Jesus, Dakota, enough," he says, downing the rest of his drink before pouring another. "I'm trying to do something for us, and all you do is question me. Do you even care?"

"I do care; I just want to talk about this, like you said. Harry, you never asked me if this was something I wanted too. This is a big step." I protest.

"Stop talking," he snaps, slamming his hands on the table.

"I'm sorry," I quickly say, feeling defeated as I look down. Suddenly, Harry throws his glass against the wall. It shatters, and I flinch, wrapping my arms around myself.

With a deep sigh, Harry glares at me with an intense anger that makes me feel small and helpless. His hands are firm on the counter, trapping me in place as he speaks, his voice thick with frustration. "I wanted to do something special for you, something that would bring us closer together, and you just had to ruin it." I can feel his breath on my face, and I can sense the disappointment that radiates from him.

"I'm sorry," I manage to say, my voice cracking under the weight of his anger. Harry steps back, rubbing his face with his hands, and turns his back to me.

"You can leave," he finally says, his voice cold and distant as he disappears toward the bedroom, leaving me standing there alone and confused.

I march down the street, battling with my jacket sleeve and muttering curses under my breath.

This damn jacket! My frustration knows no bounds as I spin the garment around a few times before finally slipping it on. Despite the biting cold, I'm a raging inferno from within. I aggressively fasten the buttons before continuing my march down the road.

As I reach the end of the street, I pace back and forth while ordering an Uber, still fuming. I begin to second-guess myself:

Am I overreacting?

No,

I can't be.

My hands tremble in the frigid air. Is it the cold, or is it the intense frustration that makes me want to hurl things across the street?

Is this why people start smoking? I wouldn't blame them if it were.

I need to calm down.

I shut my eyes and envision myself standing atop a mountain, feeling the crisp breeze and basking in the tranquility. Taking a deep breath, I attempt to calm my racing thoughts and steady my grip on my phone. The wait for my Uber seems like an eternity as I stand there alone in the cold. I keep waiting for Harry to come running down the street to apologize and tell me that he overreacted. I keep waiting and waiting, but he never shows up. Eventually, I climb into the Uber with a stranger who is silent.

Finally, I arrive home and collapse onto the couch, my mind still racing with thoughts of what happened tonight. I sit in the darkness, brooding over the events of the evening, trying to make sense of it all.

You can leave echoes in my mind, and I can feel my anger and frustration building up inside me once again.

My emotions make it difficult to think clearly.

The days slip away with no word from Harry, no calls, no surprises, nothing. It's as if he never existed, just a figment of my exhausted imagination.

At work, I stare blankly at my assignments, occasionally receiving sympathetic glances from Denise. Even running into Barbara at the store offers no comfort, as her icy reception match Harry's.

'Horrible' doesn't begin to describe how I feel. I've scoured Sian's Facebook, only to find pictures of Harry leaving a few days after our fight. Other than that, I'm completely in the dark.

And just like that, days turn into weeks, leaving me without any sense of closure.

As I wait for Zoe to arrive, I sink into the comfortable embrace of my couch and allow my mind to drift into a sea of thoughts. The weight of all the events still lingers within me, and I can feel mental exhaustion slowly creeping up. The desire for my mind to find a moment of stillness is strong, yet I'm uncertain where to begin in sorting through my feelings or how to make sense of the chaos that has been in my life lately.

Despite the uncertainty, I give myself permission to simply sit and be lost in my own world of contemplation. Finally, Zoe's voice echoes through my house, "Ding dong bitch!" followed by a barrage of knocks. I chuckle and playfully respond, "I'm sorry, you have the wrong address," before swinging the door open. We embrace each other tightly, and I realize that even though it's been years since I've seen her, this moment is exactly what I need. I hug her a little tighter than expected, feeling a sense of security that I so desperately need in her presence. I don't need to overthink or explain anything; I can just be myself around her.

The relief is real, and before I know it, tears are streaming down my face.

Zoe senses my distress and asks, "Are you okay?" She

embraces me tighter as if she knows exactly what I need. I manage to nod and sniffle, wiping my tears away with my hand. She looks me in the eyes, frowning with concern, and places her hands on my face. "Are you sure?" she asks.

I nod again, trying to compose myself, and she offers a reassuring smile. After putting her bag down, she surveyes my living room, taking in all the odd trinkets and decorations. "Happy to see you haven't lost your weird taste in decor," she says with a laugh, picking up a ceramic bowl shaped like a face. She taps the tooth and chuckles before putting it back in place.

"How was your trip here?"

"I took a train; it was weird." She laughs; she leans against my counter, giving me a small smile. "We really don't have to go out tonight if you're not feeling up to it."

"No," I blurt out, feeling the need for a night out. "I want to go."

Zoe's smile widens at the sight of the eager Dakota. Finally, her friend was starting to return to her usual self. "But first, let's go on a hike and vent our little fucking hearts out," she suggests.

We reach the top of the mountain, our breaths ragged, and hands on our hips as we stare out toward the breathtaking view. Zoe looks at me and grins before removing her backpack and pulling out a bottle of wine. "I think we've earned this," she says, patting the ground beside her. I join her with a chuckle, and she hands me the bottle. "You break the seal."

As we each take sips from the bottle, Zoe asks me about what happened.

"What exactly did he say?"

"You can leave," I say in a terrible, deep British accent.

"Jesus. What was he thinking?" Zoe exclaims, taking another sip. "Like you're really just going to leave everything and go to China? Fucking China. Imagine."

"I don't know. Maybe I'm wrong. Maybe it was his grand romantic gesture or something. I know he wants what's good for me," I say, unsure if I really know this.

Zoe looks at me in shock. "What's good for you?" she repeats incredulously.

"Yeah?" I respond hesitantly.

"The same man who pretended to be upset after actually upsetting you the same day you two fucked for the first time?" Zoe points out.

"Fucked," I repeat, cringing at her blunt language. "You make it sound so harsh."

"Well, D, the way you explained it didn't really sound like the two of you made love, ever." she retorts.

"He was offended; maybe he wanted to *fuck it out*."

"Oh please, he was offended by you saying that you didn't want to be a 'housewife.' If he wanted to 'fuck it out,' he definitely wants what's good for him." A small frown graces her face as she bites her bottom lip, contemplating whether to share her next thoughts. "Listen, D, I understand. You've always had this beautiful, hopeful heart, and that's a wonderful quality. But it's important to recognize when someone isn't good for you." Her words sink in, urging me to reflect on the situation. With genuine care in her eyes, she continues, "The way he smashes things and invades your privacy by going through your phone—it's unacceptable."

"But do I really want to be single again? At this point in my life, at this age?" I ask, my voice ting with defeat and uncertainty.

"This age?" She retorts, a hint of frustration coloring her tone. "Are we suddenly eighty years old? There's absolutely nothing wrong with choosing to be single, especially when being in a relationship means settling for someone who embodies so many warning signs." With a solemn expression, she turns toward me, her gaze piercing through mine, making sure I am fully present for her next words. "As your best friend, I will always be honest with you, and I don't believe Harry is the right fit for you, let alone capable of understanding what's truly best for you. The constant love bombing and the inability to have a constructive conversation without it spiraling into a fight—it's toxic as fuck. These are the undeniable red flags."

As the words escape her lips and fill the air, their weight sinks into my consciousness, and I can't help but acknowledge the sheer absurdity of it all. How did I allow myself to be caught up in this situation? Why didn't I recognize the supposed glaring red flags? Doubt starts to creep in, and I can't help but wonder if there's something inherently flawed within me.

A wave of guilt washes over me, "I'm sorry," I find myself muttering. The weight of responsibility and self-blame feels heavy on my shoulders.

Zoe's reaction is immediate and fills with a mix of frustration and disbelief. Her head snaps toward me, and she throws her hands up in the air, exasperated. "You did not just apologize! Stop right there. You have absolutely nothing to apologize for. Falling for a man's charming bullshit is not a crime unique to you. You're not alone in this, and it certainly isn't your fault."

Her words carry a fierce determination, a steadfast refusal to let me shoulder unnecessary blame. She refuses to let me believe that I'm somehow responsible for the situation I find myself in.

Her words are like a balm, soothing the self-doubt and guilt that had begun to gnaw at me.

I sigh and lean my head against the rock behind me. Zoe slips the bottle back into my hands and studies my face. She then places her head beside mine.

"I've known you for a long time, D, and big city life has never been your thing. Trust me, as someone who was actually born there, I can confidently say that China wouldn't have been a good fit for you. And let's not forget the fact that he's ghosting you right now, after all the nonsense he put you through. It's just unbelievably gross. Being single is okay; forget about your age; this isn't the 1900s, where you have to be barefoot and pregnant and married to a man who is abusive."

I let out a deep sigh, taking her words in. I reach for the bottle of wine, take a generous sip, and we sit together in a moment of contemplative silence.

Eventually, Zoe breaks the stillness, determine to shift our focus.

"All right, enough of this. We need to get ready. We're meeting the ship folk at eight," Zoe declares, her voice fill with determination.

"All right, all right," I groan playfully, allowing her to take hold of my hands and lift me off the ground. With a firm grip on my shoulders, she flashes a bright smile and declares, "Tonight, we're going to have the most incredible time."

8

Zoe and I relished in the excitement of getting ready for a night out. The perfect playlist filled the room as we debated on outfits, did each others' hair, and perfected our makeup. With Zoe by my side, laughter and comfort came effortlessly, as if it were second nature.

The drive to the bar was filled with boisterous laughter and nostalgic music, our excitement palpable. As we parked near the entrance and grab our coats, Zoe proclaims, "I'll be the designated driver tonight. I'll sober up before we leave." She hooks her arm into mine, and we stroll toward the door, IDs in hand. The bouncer greets us with a smile as we make our way inside.

Zoe's friends were waiting for us at a cozy booth in the back, and as we approach, they cheer our arrival. "Calm down, guys," Zoe teases. "This is Dakota. Dakota, meet Israel, Dwayne, Nicole, and Logan." We exchange warm smiles and waves as we sit down. I slide into the open spot next to Logan, and Zoe follows suit.

"So, do you all work in the same department?" I ask as I settle in, slipping my bag behind my back along with my jacket.

"We do, but Logan here is from shoreside," Nicole explains, her eyes rolling as she playfully nudges Logan. He laughs, clearly used to the banter.

"Shoreside?" I ask, intrigued by the unfamiliar term.

Logan grins, his eyes sparkling mischievously. "Yeah, I only come on board every now and again to make sure these guys do their jobs," he jokes, eliciting more laughter from the group.

I watch him, fascinated by his job. "So you don't stay onboard for months like they do?" I ask, accepting a drink from Zoe and settling back in my chair.

"No, I usually just stay for a few weeks and then fly to the next ship. But this is my last ship before vacation, so I get to walk off and go home in a few days before the ship departs."

"Oh, you're from London?"

"I am," Logan says with a smirk, leaning closer to me and resting his elbows on the table. "And I heard you're from here too."

I nod, taking another sip of my drink. "Well, not London. I live in Shere."

"I'm from Honduras," Israel chimes in proudly, "Nic is from the Philippines, and Dwayne boy over here is from Jamaica, and we all get to hang out tonight," Zoe laughs. "Pretty cool, huh?"

Zoe's chatter about Shere charm was a welcome distraction from Logan's intense gaze on me. I squirm in my seat, the uncomfortable feeling of his stare intensifying as he leans closer to me, his hand creeping up my thigh; I jolt back in surprise, my heart racing with discomfort. His dark smirk sends shivers down my spine, and I can't shake the feeling that something is off with him.

Way off.

"I'm really looking forward to getting to know you, Dakota," he whispers, his warm breath sending a chill through my body. The sudden shift in his demeanor left me feeling uneasy and uncomfortable.

Desperate to escape the situation, I jolt up, causing everyone to look at me. "Sorry," I laugh nervously, "I really need to pee." I cringe at my words, sensing Zoe's suspicious stare. Quickly, I make my way toward the restroom signs, desperate for a moment to collect myself and shake off the discomfort that still lingers after Logan's advances. I close the door behind me and take a deep breath, letting the cool air fill my lungs. Washing my hands, I feel the droplets of water trickling down my arms, trying to calm the unease that still lingers within me.

Leaving the restroom, I make my way to the bar, feeling the need for something stronger than beer or cider. Luckily, a group of people blocks the booth's view, giving me some privacy. I find an open spot at the bar and patiently wait for my turn to order.

After a brief moment, the bartender catches sight of me, and I promptly place an order for something strong; as I wait for my drink to be made, I allow my gaze to wander across the sea of unfamiliar faces surrounding me. The sheer number of strangers in this bustling place momentarily overwhelms me, and I take a deep breath, attempting to quell the rising waves of panic that threaten to consume me.

Yet, just as anxiety starts to tighten its grip, a spark of recognition ignites within me. Across the bar, amidst the lively crowd, I spot a face that brings instant relief. It's a familiar face, belonging to someone who surprisingly holds a special place in my heart. A warm sensation washes over me, and my tense body immediately eases as I observe him engrossed in conversation with a group of friends. His genuine laughter fills the air, and with each sip of his drink, he nods along attentively, fully engaged in the moment.

With a faint smile lingering on my lips, I briefly avert my gaze, savoring the moment of quiet admiration. As I turn my attention back toward him, our eyes meet in an instant of perfect connection. There's a pause, a beat suspends in time before a soft chuckle escapes his lips, and he shakes his head in disbelief. He exchanges a few words with his friends, his eyes never wavering from mine, before gracefully maneuvering through the crowd, making his way toward me.

"Heathcliff," he greets, his voice fill with familiarity and warmth as he places a tender kiss on my cheek, his arm gently finding its place on the counter.

"Hi," I reply, my voice laced with a hint of delight that I can't quite contain. The uneasiness that had previously enveloped me completely evaporates, replaced by genuine happiness at the sight of him.

"It's been a while. You look good," he remarks, his eyes scanning my face with appreciation.

A playful grin curves my lips as I tease, "So do you. Finally embracing a more relaxed style, I see."

His laughter fills the air, a melodic sound that makes my heart dance. He leans in closer, his gaze locks with mine as if we're the only two people in the room.

"How are you?" he asks, his voice ting with genuine concern.

I take my drink from the bartender and meet his gaze once again, feeling a mixture of vulnerability and comfort in his presence.

"I'm good," I begin, allowing a small smile to grace my lips. "Yeah, good. And how about you?"

Noah's piercing gaze narrows as if he can see right through me. "Where's Harry?" he asks, his tone fills with curiosity.

I let out a sigh, rubbing my temple with a wistful chuckle. "Well, I think we broke up."

"You *think* you broke up?" he echoes, his confusion evident.

I furrow my brow, momentarily lost in a maze of contemplation, and shift my focus toward the counter. Resting my hands around my drink, I seek solace in its cool surface, hoping for a moment of grounding amidst the storm of emotions.

"You know, I'm not entirely sure what's going on, to be honest," I confess, finding a sense of relief in opening up to him. He regards me with a solemn expression, his gaze penetrating mine, and a moment of silence descends between us as if inviting me to share what's on my mind. But I'm at a loss for words, so I let out a nervous chuckle and say, "I'm sorry," my eyes darting downwards in embarrassment.

Noah nods understandingly, his eyes fills with empathy, and he places a comforting hand on my arm. I feel a gentle reassurance emanating from his touch, easing the weight on my shoulders. As I lift my gaze to meet his, a mixture of concern and genuine care is reflecting in his eyes.

"You know," he says with a soft smile, "I happen to be a really good listener." His words are accompanied by a playful wink, infusing the moment with a touch of lightheartedness. I release a sigh, feeling the warmth of his touch seep into my being.

"You might as well start charging me for these therapy sessions," I quip, attempting to lighten the mood.

He smiles at my remark and takes hold of my hand, leading me away from the bustling bar toward a quieter corner. With a quick text to Zoe, informing her of my whereabouts, Noah and I settle into our seats.

"Jesus," Noah shakes his head in disbelief after I poured my heart out, leaving nothing unsaid about Harry. Noah's piercing gaze softens as he takes a deep breath, trying to choose his words carefully. "Dakota," he says gently, "before I offer any advice, I need to know if you want to hear it or if you just needed to vent." His sincerity catches me off guard, leaving me speechless for a moment.

After a pause, I let out a nervous chuckle and apologize for my indecisiveness. "I'm sorry," I say, not sure what I actually want at that moment.

Noah's warm eyes meet mine again as he spoke, "You need to stop apologizing when you did nothing wrong." His expression is soft.

I meet his eyes and nod. "You're right," I admit, feeling a sense of relief wash over me. "Tell me what you honestly think," I say. Noah's eyes peer deeply into mine as he sighs, taking my hand and pulling it gently between us to ensure I focus on him.

Noah's gentle grasp on my hand was reassuring as he spoke his honest thoughts. "I think the fact that I have never seen you truly happy around him speaks volumes," he admits, his soft eyes still lock onto mine. I feel a lump form in my throat as I absorb his words. He squeezes my hand gently, offering me comfort. "But," he continues, "I also think that nothing I say matters because, at the end of the day, it is your choice on what you want to do."

"I don't know what to do." My voice is barely above a whisper Noah nods understandingly, his warm eyes reflecting his empathy.

"Take all the time you need, Dakota. You don't have to figure everything out today. Just focus on doing what's best for you right now."

His grip on my hand is reassuring as I chuckle and wipe away some tears with my free hand, feeling a bit embarrassed for breaking down in a bar.

"I promise I won't tell anyone," Noah quips with a wink, handing me a napkin to clean myself up. A grateful smile graces my lips as I soak in the warmth of his presence. I consider inviting him to join us, but he's with his friends, and I don't know Zoe's friends well enough to make introductions, so I let out a resigned sigh and begin to pull away.

"I should probably head back to Zoe," I murmur, my gaze shifting downward to our joined hands, a tender connection that holds a depth of appreciation toward Noah. The genuine sense of gratitude that flows between us serves as a reminder of the significance of his support. Sincerity colors my voice as I express it, "Thank you, Noah."

He returns my smile, pressing a gentle kiss to my hand before releasing it. As I stand up to leave, he calls out to me, stopping me in my tracks.

"Here," he offers, handing me his card. I take it from him, studying the details on the card. His name and phone number stare back at me, almost as if they're smiling. I look up at Noah, feeling a sense of appreciation for his kindness.

"Thank you," I say again, smiling as I turn to make my way back to Zoe in the booth.

Zoe's smile brightens as I slide into the booth beside her, but I can't help but avoid eye contact with Logan. Trying to shake off the awkwardness, I joke, "What did I miss?"

Israel chuckles and replies, "We were just talking about American politics."

"Hard pass for me," I reply, scrunching up my nose.

Dwayne nods in agreement, adding, "See? Nothing good ever comes from talking about religion or politics."

Nicole teases, "And here I was about to ask you guys what religion you follow," winking at Zoe and causing them both to laugh.

Israel breaks the laughter by suggesting, "Who's ready for the next round of drinks?"

"I got this one," I announce, met with cheers from the group. After taking their orders, I make my way toward the bar, eager to place the orders. As I scan the bustling surroundings, a flicker of hope ignites within me, wishing to spot Noah still present, perhaps even considering inviting him and his friends to join us this time. However, my search yields no sign of him, and a sense of disappointment settles in.

Determine to fulfill my task, I redirect my attention and focus on the matter at hand. With a composed demeanor, I relay the drink orders to the bartender; suddenly, a pair of hands slither around my waist, accompanied by the pungent scent of alcohol on their breath. Startle, I turn to find Logan, his grip tightening as he pulls me closer to him. A wave of discomfort washes over me, and I instinctively try to create some distance, but his hold remains firm.

"Logan, please stop touching me," I assert, my voice carrying a firm tone, hoping he would respect my boundaries.

He pouts, seemingly undeterred by my request, and presses his body even closer, disregarding my plea. Determine to assert myself, I push him away with more force this time. "No, I'm not interested. I'm sorry," I emphasize, hoping that he will finally back off.

However, my words fall on deaf ears. Ignoring my clear rejection, he once again grabs my waist, his touch growing more forceful as he leans into my neck, his fingers digging uncomfortably into my skin.

"I'll make you interested," he declares before sucking on the skin below my ear. I freeze, feeling trapped.

He finally lets go and grabs three drinks before disappearing towards the booth.

Feeling sick to my stomach, I grab the remaining drinks and head towards the booth, where Zoe stands up to help me. I shoot her a look, and she nods, understanding.

"Dakota, can you show me where the toilets are?" she asks, and I'm relieved for the excuse to escape the situation.

"Ugh, fucking Logan," she groans, pacing up and down as I sit on the sink counter after recounting the incident to her. "He's so used to getting whatever girl he wants on the ship. I should have known he'd try to get with you, too. That man would sleep with anything that has a hole." I chuckle at her words, swaying my legs as she turns to me, taking my hands in hers. "I'm so sorry, D. He rarely comes out with us, but we were the only option as the rest of the staff is working. Shoreside managers don't really have friends on ships since they're always traveling. Do you want me to talk to him?"

"No, it's fine," I say, squeezing her hands. "But I think I'll go outside for some fresh air, maybe grab something greasy and gross from the Seven-Eleven on the corner."

"Do you want me to come with you?"

"No, stay and have fun. I won't be long, and I'll bring you back something gross and greasy, too," I say, smiling before she hugs me tightly. "Zoe, I'll be okay. This is London; the streets will be full of people and loads of witnesses," I joke, patting her on the back.

"Okay, but just keep your phone on you." She sighs before giving me another hug.

The cool breeze kisses my face as I stroll past the barely lit park cars lining the bar entrance. A feeling of relief washes over me as I spot my trusty old car sitting in the same spot where I left it. Suddenly, I hear footsteps approaching from behind, and my heart skips a beat. Fearing the worst, I quickly dart behind the nearest car, praying to the gods that it's not Logan.

As I try to make myself as small as possible, my heart beating fast in my chest, a laugh breaks through my panic, and I look up to see who it is. "Heathcliff, what on earth are you doing?" Noah chuckles as he watches me hiding behind a car. I laugh with relief as I struggle to get up. He offers his hand, and I gratefully take it as he pulls me to my feet.

"If you must know, I was hiding," I say with a grin.

"Well, that's a terrible hiding spot," he quips, his eyes wandering to my icy hands. "And your hands are like literal ice blocks."

"I'm sorry my hiding spot isn't the Tristan Da Cunha of hiding spots, Mr. Darcy," I retort, adjusting my skirt. "I was out of options."

Noah chuckles at my banter. "My car is just up here. Would you like to warm up while you hide?"

Yes, please," I exclaim, eagerly following him. He opens the door for me, taking my hand as he helps me into the car. With a flick of a switch, the engine roars to life, and warm air floods the interior. We both sink into the backseat, heads resting on the headrests, basking in the heat.

"I can finally feel my toes slowly defrosting," I murmur, relishing the warmth.

Noah turns to me, his kind eyes curious. "What are you hiding from anyway?"

"Ugh," I groan, turning to face him. "One of Zoe's ship friends. He's a bit too persistent for my liking."

"Too much liquid courage?" Noah suggests, a hint of amusement in his voice.

I chuckle, staring at the ceiling. "Way too much."

"It's really nice seeing you like this," Noah says, smiling.

I turn to him, my own smile widening. "Like what?"

"Almost carefree," he replies, his eyes fix on mine. "It suits you."

I savor his words, letting them linger in my mind for a moment before a smile spreads across my face. Noah has always been beautiful, no doubt about that, but it was never just about his physical appearance. It was the way his eyes could soothe me in a room full of strangers, his kind and supportive personality.

The realization washes over me like a wave as I gaze into his smiling eyes. The banter, the sense of security, the never-ending laughter and serious conversations, and just the act of being here with him – it all hits me like a ton of bricks. And suddenly, I'm struck with the realization that this could be something I would want to do for the rest of my life.

With him.

In a sudden moment of abandon, I act on my impulse and reach for him, my fingers curling around the side of his face. I don't pause to consider the consequences or potential pitfalls of my actions as my lips crash into his, lost in the passion of the moment. At first, he's stunned, frozen, but it's short-lived as his hands find my waist, pulling me onto his lap. I bury my fingers in his curly hair as our tongues tangle and battle for control.

But as quickly as it starts, Noah pulls away, breathless and uncertain. "Dakota, wait," he says, tenderly brushing my hair back from my face, his hand on my waist disappearing. "Are you sure? We had drinks and...."

"Noah," I reassure him, my voice steady and clear. I see the uncertainty in his eyes as he scans my face, looking for any sign that I might be under the influence. But as I lean closer, my hands on his face, tracing the lines of his jaw, he seems to relax.

"I'm sure," I whisper, my eyes locks onto his. And with that, I kiss him again, this time with less urgency but no less passion.

Soon enough, his hands are back on my body, tracing the curves of my skin as we undress each other with gentle urgency.

He flips me over onto my back with graceful ease, the leather couch accepting my body as if it was made for it. With nimble fingers, I unbutton his shirt as he presses his hand beside me, making sure his weight doesn't crush me. His other hand runs up my leg, teasingly pulling at my stockings.

Finally reaching the end of his buttons, I sweep his shirt off his shoulders, and he laughs against my mouth, his warm breath sending shivers down my spine. "Your hands are still so cold," he says in between kisses, but the playful tone in his voice brings a smile to my lips. As my fingers trace his abs on his stomach, I can feel the goosebumps rising under my touch, and we both start laughing together, the sound filling the car with a joyous melody.

He comes to a halt, his gaze fixed on me as he reaches out to brush his thumb gently across my cheek, down to my lips. Our eyes lock, and I can feel my heart pounding with anticipation. I close my eyes, savoring the sensation of his touch.

"Look at me," he whispers, and I obey, my eyes fluttering open to meet his gaze once more. It's as though I'm seeing him again for the first time, and I'm struck by how incredibly beautiful he is. My body responds to his proximity, and I can feel the heat rising within me.

With a smile, he leans down to kiss me again, and everything else fades away in a burst of euphoria and I never want it to end.

I lay comfortably on his chest as we share endless laughter over our shared stories, our clothes scattered around the car, and our legs intertwined while he strokes my back. Our conversation flows naturally, and there's no hint of discomfort or regret in the air.

Suddenly, my phone chimes with a message, reminding me of the outside world. I let out a sigh, and Noah sits up, gently caressing my cheek.

"It's probably Zoe," he says.

"Can't we just stay here?" I plead, sinking deeper into his touch.

He chuckles. "As much as I'd love that, Zoe might get more worried."

Another message interrupts our moment, and I glance at my bag before turning back to Noah. "Five more minutes?" I suggest before kissing him again. But the message tone pings again, and I groan as Noah laughs and hands me my bag.

"It's all right. We have plenty of time," he assures me with a smile.

"I'm sorry," I say with a sigh, but Noah's eyes soften as he cups my face in his hands and kisses me gently.

"Please stop apologizing," he whispers between kisses.

I step out of Noah's car, feeling the cool night air against my skin. He gives me a warm smile as I turn to face him, and I can't help but wrap my arms around his neck. He envelops me in a warm and tender embrace, his chin finding a resting place on my shoulder.

"Please let me know when you get home safely, yeah?" he murmurs softly as we reluctantly release our embrace. His words carry a sincere tone, reflecting his genuine care for my well-being. He releases me slowly, his fingers lingering on the collar of my shirt under my sweater, adjusting it with a gentle touch.

I nod and start making my way toward the bar entrance, but I can't resist turning back to look at him. He's leaning against his car, his eyes lock onto mine. I walk back toward him, and he meets me halfway, his arms encircling my waist.

"One more for the road?" I playfully suggest, a smile dancing on my lips. He chuckles in response, his hands tenderly caressing my face as he leans in for another kiss, the warmth of his lips against mine intensifying the bittersweet moment.

"Good night, Heathcliff," he whispers, his voice fill with a hint of longing.

"Good night, Mr. Darcy," I reply, unable to suppress the smile that creeps onto my face. With each step I take as I walk away, I can sense his gaze lingering on me, a mixture of affection and longing until I'm finally out of sight.

9

After successfully avoiding Logan, Zoe and I finally make it back to my place. We both sink into the plush comfort of my bed, the gentle embrace of the mattress providing solace to my restless mind. I send a quick text to Noah, assuring him of my safe arrival home, before setting my phone aside. Zoe lies beside me, absorbed in her own device, and after a moment, I gather the courage to speak up.

"You are right," I confess, a sense of relief accompanying my words.

Zoe's face lights up with a mischievous grin, her phone resting on her chest. "Oh, do tell," she playfully prompts, eager to hear my revelation.

"Harry is not good for me," I admit with newfound clarity. "I'm done with all of that."

"Took you long enough," she teases, her tone lightheart. "So, what's next?"

I gather my thoughts, a flame of determination flickering within me, illuminating my path forward. "I refuse to linger in the past," I assert, my voice lace with newfound strength. "I guess I'm choosing to move on because dwelling on what was will only hinder anything that could come. It's time for a fresh start."

Zoe's expression shifts to one of concern, her brows furrowing with worry.

"And what if he comes back?" she asks, her voice ting with uncertainty. I shake my head resolutely.

"I honestly don't know," I admit, my tone ting with a hint of vulnerability. "Our relationship was already unhealthy, and communicating was difficult even before he left; I can't imagine it being better if he does decide to show back up. It doesn't make sense to try to discuss anything with him when he won't listen. I guess I'll just cross that weird bridge when I get to it."

Zoe's face softens with empathy as she reaches out to hold my hand, a gesture of support. "I'm so proud of you for making this decision, even without the closure you may have hoped for."

"Thanks, Zoe," I smile, holding onto her hand tightly. "I wish you could stay longer."

"Me too. Overnight stays are so rare. I'm just glad we got to have one here," she says with a smile.

"Can I drive you to the train station tomorrow?" I ask, hoping to spend a little more time with her.

"Absolutely." Her face lights up with a broad grin as she eagerly states, "Now, tell me everything about Noah!"

I chuckle before divulging every detail, starting from the first time I met him up until our encounter in his car; after taking a moment to reflect on everything, I must confess that I'm feeling absolutely terrible.

"I think that my impulsive actions may have jeopardized our friendship. While I would love to spend more time with him and to get to know him even more, I understand that the timing may not be right given the Harry situation. And I would hate for these feelings I have for him to be one-sided."

"Do you have any regrets about what happened?"

"Absolutely not. In fact, I feel giddy just thinking about it; it was amazing. The way it just felt… good. Not just the sex itself but everything. It felt like I had sex with Noah, and I know that makes no sense, but with Harry, it always felt so…angry. Like I was having sex with someone completely different, there were never any sweet moments where we could just be ourselves and enjoy each other. You know, like laughing or just being human. It was always so intense and rough. And the moment it was all over, it was like he became Harry again."

"I understand. Rough sex can be great when the timing is right, but we all deserve moments of tenderness and intimacy, too."

"Exactly," I sigh, my gaze drifting up to the ceiling. As if she possesses an uncanny ability to understand the desires of my heart, Zoe sits up and turns toward me.

"Noah truly does sound like a genuinely good and caring person, D," she remarks, her words offering a glimmer of comfort. "He sounds patient, and he listens to you. And I know these are practically bare minimum traits, but the way you look when you talk about him, you look so calm and happy."

"I feel calm and happy; there is no storm erupting in my stomach around him, and I really like that," I reply, my nervousness causing me to bite my lip. "I suppose I'm just worried that I may have driven him away or perhaps damaged our friendship by allowing him to be caught up in my impulsive moment."

"No, I highly doubt it," she reassures me, a smile gracing her lips. "It appears that he, dare I say, understands you, Heathcliff," she teases, lightening the mood.

Standing outside my car at the train station, Zoe's bag securely resting on her back, we exchange a sad smile before embracing each other. As we hold on tight, she whispers,

"Please stay safe." I nod, reciprocating the hug, before we finally let go and smile at each other. "I love you, D," Zoe says with a genuine affection that warms my heart.

"I love you too," I respond, my voice lace with emotions as a lump forms in my throat. As she turns her gaze toward the ready to depart train, its resonating horn piercing the air, I follow her line of sight and catch a glimpse of Logan, lost in his own world with his luggage, oblivious to our presence. She rolls her eyes, a clear message of disdain, but her expression quickly shifts into one of significance.

"Forget about that jerk," she asserts, her voice fill with determination. "And don't overanalyze things with Noah, okay? Just let things unfold naturally. He genuinely does seem like someone who would be good for you, but regardless of what happens, remember that you *will* be okay. With or without a man." She reassures me as if she can effortlessly perceive the thoughts racing through my mind. Nodding in agreement, I offer a smile as she waves goodbye and gracefully walks away.

Alone once again, I settle into my car and drive back to Shere, finding solace in the familiar streets. Before heading home, I decide to make a quick stop at the store since my shelves were looking a bit bare.

Guiding my trolley through the aisles, I take my time, leisurely browsing the items on display as I contemplate a cake mix. A subtle sensation tugs at my awareness as if someone's gaze is fixed upon me. I glance around, but there's no one in immediate sight paying attention to anything other than the goods in their hands, so I shrug it off and continue my shopping.

Just as I reach for another flavor of cake mix, a gentle brush against my hand startles me, causing me to retract instinctively.

"Sorry," I murmur, turning to face the person responsible.

Logan, standing before me. Surprise and nerves intertwine in my voice as I ask, "What are you doing here?"

He offers a smile, lifting a lingering hand on my cheek. I instinctively take a step back, creating a small barrier between us with the trolley.

"You mentioned Shere last night, and I thought I'd check it out. It's quite charming," he replies, his touch still nagging on my skin. He leans forward, resting his hands on the trolley's handle, and continues, "Look, I was drunk last night. I'm used to things being fast-paced. You understand that, right?"

I hold his gaze, my eyes narrowing slightly, and inquire, "So, you followed me here just to tell me this?"

A wide grin spreads across his face. "Well, you didn't give me your number," he quips playfully.

Feeling the weight of the situation, I quickly survey the store, grateful for the presence of other customers. Realizing that I can always come back later, I step back decisively, locking eyes with Logan, who watches my every move.

"I believe I made myself clear last night," I assert with unwavering firmness before turning away. My pace quickens as I navigate through the aisles, heading toward the exit. My fingers fumble in my bag, desperately searching for my car keys; my trembling hands feel as though they're coated in slick coconut oil, causing everything to slip from my grasp. After what feels like an eternity, I manage to extract my keys from my bag, their metallic jingle providing a fleeting moment of reassurance.

However, before I can even attempt to unlock my car door, a sudden force pushes me against it, pressing me firmly. Logan's face buries into the skin of my neck, eliciting a shiver down my spine. In the chaos of the moment, my keys slip from my grasp, clattering to the ground, their significance momentarily forgotten.

"Please, wait," I plead, but Logan only smiles against my neck, turning me around before pinning me back against my car.

"Oh, Dakota, I really enjoy it when you beg," he whispers, his lips tracing a path to my jaw. A passing couple gives us a side-eye before quickly disappearing into the store, and a few raindrops cascade down, mingling with the racing beats of my heart.

Taking a deep breath, I attempt to steady my racing pulse,

my eyes searching for clarity as I meet Logan's gaze, hoping to find some semblance of understanding amidst this tumultuous situation.

His grip on my waist tightens, constricting like an iron vice, and I summon every ounce of strength within me to push him away. My palms press firmly against his chest, but his hands instinctively seize mine, refusing to release their hold, desperate to maintain control.

"Please, stop," I manage to utter, my voice barely a whisper, as I struggle against his overpowering grasp. The weight of his grip intensifies, squeezing my hands with an unforgiving force. My fingers throb with pain, their vulnerability overwhelmed by the pressure.

His sneering voice cuts through the air, laden with disdain and accusation. "You have a boyfriend, don't you? Is it the guy from the bar?" His scowl twists his features into a grotesque mask of resentment, jealousy, and possessiveness.

With every fiber of my being, I attempt to break free, to pull away from his clutches, but he tightens his grip even more, his hold growing more suffocating. "Logan, you're hurting me," I plead, my voice trembling with a mixture of fear and pain.

In a sudden burst of aggression, he shoves me away forcefully, propelling me back against my car. My heart hammers against my ribcage, the thud echoing in my ears as a surge of adrenaline courses through my veins. I know I must escape this dangerous situation, and I take a step back, then another, creating distance between us.

Rubbing his temple in apparent contemplation, his next move uncertain, I seize the opportunity. A surge of determination pushes me forward, my legs propelling me into a sprint. Each footfall reverberates against the pavement, the rhythm of my escape, as I strive to put as much distance as possible between myself and the menacing presence of Logan.

Rain lashes against my face, each droplet merging with my tears as I sprint desperately toward the safety of my home. My heart pounds in my burning chest as I reach my street, my vision blurred by the cascading rain.

To my dismay, a car sits ominously parked in front of my house. Through the downpour, I struggle to identify the figure inside, praying to the gods that it's not Logan.

How would he even know where I live?

Ignoring the racing thoughts in my mind, I focus on one thing—I need to reach the sanctuary of my home. As I draw closer, the figure emerges from the car and begins to chase after me. Panic surges through my veins, urging my burning legs to carry me faster. But my efforts prove futile as they catch up to me, seizing me forcefully by the waist and slamming me against their body.

A scream escapes my lips, muffled by the rain-soaked air as I thrash and struggle, desperately fighting to break free from their grip. But then, their hand grasps my face, forcing me to meet their gaze.

The sight that meets my bewildered eyes leaves me speechless as I drown out their panicked words.

What the fuck?

Harry?

Confusion and disorientation wash over me as I tentatively reach out to touch his face, trying to make sense of the surreal situation unfolding before me. My body, overwhelmed by the whirlwind of emotions and events, succumbs to exhaustion, and I collapse onto my knees, sobbing uncontrollably as he holds me tightly. With gentle yet firm arms, he lifts me up and carries me inside, providing a much-needed refuge from the storm raging both outside and within me. Relief floods my being for a brief moment, as I am grateful that it's not Logan standing in front of me.

Yet, my mind remains clouded, struggling to comprehend the unaccounted presence of Harry and the madness that has ensued.

Settling me down on the couch, he swiftly removes his own drenched coat and retrieves towels from my bathroom.

My mind races with a whirlwind of questions, leaving me dizzy and overwhelmed. I glance down at my swollen, throbbing fingers, my reality teetering on the edge of disbelief.

Could this all be a hallucination, another figment of my now shattered imagination?

What is happening, and what in the actual fuck is Harry doing here?

The questions swirl relentlessly, echoing the chaos within me as I struggle to grasp the unfathomable truth of what just unfolded.

As I try to regulate my erratic breathing, my eyes widen in astonishment as Harry emerges from my room, clutching towels in his hands. Concern etches deeply into his face as he swiftly approaches, enfolding me in a tight embrace. I instinctively push back, attempting to regain control of my racing breath.

"How...how are you here?" I manage to gasp out, my voice strain with disbelief. Harry kneels in front of me, his gaze lock onto mine, searching for answers as his gentle touch brushes my wet hair away from my face.

"Dakota, what happened?" His voice carries a tinge of urgency, almost bordering on desperation. I shake my head in disbelief, still reeling from the shock, as he pulls me closer and drapes a warm towel around my trembling form. "Dakota," he says, his voice fills with concern, shaking me slightly as if trying to bring me back to reality.

"Harry," I finally manage to utter, my voice barely above a whisper. "I'm still trying to make sense of it all." The weight of the recent events bears down upon me, and the silence between us stretches, heavy with unspoken emotions. With a deep breath, I finally find the strength to gather my thoughts and recount the harrowing experience to Harry, my voice quivering and raw with the intensity of the emotions that still course through me.

10

A heavy silence settles upon the room, amplifying the tension that hangs in the air. Harry's fingers instinctively seek solace on his temple, tracing invisible paths as if trying to alleviate the mounting pressure. Restlessness takes hold of me, compelling my body to fidget, shifting anxiously from one leg to another, a physical manifestation of the inner turmoil I'm grappling with. The whirlwind of recent events has left my mind in disarray, the pace of it all overwhelming. And now, with Harry's presence in this chaotic mix, I'm confronted with another layer of complexity.

Questions swirl in my mind like a nasty storm:

Will Logan make another attempt?

Is he still lurking in the shadows of Shere, waiting for the right moment to strike?

I look up, and my gaze meets Harry's, and a surge of realization courses through me. The weight of the moment settles heavily upon my shoulders, and I come to the difficult realization that I must confront our own relationship, too, to sever the ties that bind us.

The thought of breaking up with Harry feels like stepping into the unknown, a leap of faith into uncertain territory. Yet, as the weight of this realization hangs in the air, it becomes a daunting task to find the right words to navigate the delicate terrain of ending a relationship.

Overwhelm by the sheer magnitude of this entire situation, I find myself standing on the edge of my sanity; I feel as if I'm losing grip on reality, the boundaries blurring, and my thoughts spiraling into a maddening frenzy.

My god, I am losing it.

Finally, Harry shatters the suffocating silence, jolting me back to reality. However, his words carry a bitter edge, causing a knot of tension to tighten in the pit of my stomach.

"None of this would have happened if you hadn't gone to that bar," he accuses, his anger tangible in the air. A wave of disbelief washes over me; I reel back, my mind struggling to process his accusation. My voice quivers as I respond, a mixture of shock and indignation lacing my words.

"What?"

"You heard me," he retorts, his eyes ablaze with fury.

I take a step closer, hoping to bridge the growing divide between us.

"Harry, I just wanted to spend time with my friend," I explain, my voice ting with frustration.

His gaze averts, his hands busying themselves with pouring a drink.

"You could have seen her here," he mutters, his tone lace with resentment. "None of this would have happened if you had just stayed at home."

A surge of anger courses through me, fueling my response.

"So, what? Am I supposed to confine myself to the four walls of my house forever? Is that how you envision our lives? This didn't happen because of where I chose to go but because of what he did."

Harry's jaw tightens, his words lace with frustration. "Dakota, I'm telling you that this could have been avoided if you had just listened to me."

My patience wanes, my voice growing more resolute. "Listen to you? Always stay home unless I'm with you? I am not a child, Harry."

Bitter edge colors his next words as he lashes back, "Well, you sure are acting like one."

The tension between us escalates to its breaking point, each word hanging heavily in the air, leaving a bitter taste in my mouth. Filled with a mix of frustration and disappointment, I turn, ready to escape the suffocating atmosphere. This is my house, yet at this moment, I'd rather be anywhere else.

But before I can reach the sanctuary of the door, Harry swiftly places his empty glass on the counter and steps in front of me, effectively blocking my path. His presence is both a barrier and an invitation to engage further.

"Wait," he implores, his voice softening. "I didn't mean it like that. I'm just... I'm just so angry. Can't you understand how terrified I was seeing you like that? All I want is for you to be safe." His hand reaches out, taking mine, and he presses a gentle kiss upon it. A fragile smile forms on his face as he continues, "You know that, right?"

Caught in the midst of conflicting emotions, I pause, a swirl of thoughts and doubts clouding my mind. While I appreciate Harry being here, I can't ignore the suffocating grip of overprotectiveness that has begun to strangle our relationship. I know deep down that the time for us to have a serious conversation and bring an end to our unhappy dynamic is now.

Harry's arms encircle me, pulling me into an embrace, his lips gently grazing the top of my head. "I did say that something bad might happen, didn't I? Perhaps I had an intuition. I care about you so deeply, and all I want is to ensure your safety," he murmurs his voice ting with a mix of relief and concern. Drawing back slightly, he locks eyes with me, a plea for trust etches in his gaze. "Maybe next time, just trust me when I voice my concerns, okay?" He pulls me back into the warmth of his chest, sighing softly. "I'm just so grateful that I was here for you today."

As I exhale a sigh of my own, a sigh loads with the weight

of impending change, I remain uncertain about my next words.

Harry's grip on my shoulders tightens, pulling me back toward him. A smile stretches across his face as if he's unaware of the turmoil swirling within me. "Now, get your coat. My parents are dying to meet you," he declares.

I freeze, my mind reeling from his unexpected announcement. Confusion seeps into my expression as I take a step back, trying to comprehend his words. My phone chimes repeatedly on the table nearby; Harry glances at the phone with narrow eyes before refocusing on me.

"No. I'm not going anywhere," I assert firmly, appalled by the audacity of this whole interaction.

His face contorts with a mix of surprise and frustration. "Dakota, please. I already told them we would be there tonight," he pleads, his voice fills with frustration.

"You didn't even tell me that you would be here today!" I retort, my voice louder than intended, fuelled by a sense of disbelief and anger.

He takes a step toward me, his gaze piercing mine. "I wanted to surprise you. I came home early just to do something nice for you. Can't I do something without being challenged for once?"

I look at him in disbelief; the pain in my fingers is prominent as I squeeze my hands into fists, trying desperately to contain my anger,

"Dakota, please. It'll be a great distraction," he insists, gesturing toward my room. "Go on then."

I stare at him in disbelief, the weight of his words sinking in. The surge of anger threatens to consume me, but I take a deep breath, trying to maintain my composure. I reluctantly give in, feeling defeated; I walk toward my room. The hallway feels suffocating, each step filled with resentment.

In the bathroom, I look at my reflection in the mirror, my eyes reflecting exhaustion and disappointment. The urge to call

Noah gnaws at me, seeking solace in his understanding. I resist the temptation, splashing water on my face to clear my mind. I hastily brush my teeth and tie my hair up, a sense of resignation lingering in the air.

With my coat in hand, I make my way toward the door. Harry leans against the kitchen counter, a smile etched across his face, waiting for me to join him. Reluctantly, I follow, knowing that this evening will be far from the distraction I truly need.

The ride to Harry's parents' house is accompanied by the soft hum of music, creating a serene ambiance that only amplifies the sense of anticipation lingering in the air. We arrive at a picturesque cottage, its charm accentuated by the surrounding landscape. Harry turns off the car engine and turns to me, seeking reassurance.

"Ready?" he asks, his gaze filled with a mixture of hope and uncertainty. I muster a small, forced smile, masking my true emotions. As Harry opens his door, he suddenly pauses, reaching into his pocket and retrieving my phone. "Oh, here. You almost forgot it at home," he says, handing it to me before stepping out of the car. I glance at the lock screen and furrow my brow, noting the absence of any new messages despite hearing the notification sound earlier. My thoughts on the phone are interrupted as Harry opens my door and takes the lead, guiding us toward the front door. The tantalizing aroma of savory curry greets us, enveloping the air with its delicious scent.

As Harry helps me out of my coat, gracefully hanging it among the others on the wall, his voice echoes through the hallway, announcing our arrival. The sound of footsteps on the polished wooden floors draws closer, and soon enough, Harry's mother emerges.

"Harry, my darling boy, welcome home!" she exclaims, her eyes lighting up as she caresses his face and places a loving kiss on his cheek. "Come, come. You must be exhausted. How was China? And when are you and Dakota planning to go back? I want to hear all about your adventures."

"I'll share all the details soon, Mother," Harry replies, stealing a glance at me and flashing a playful grin. "Oh, and this is Dakota. Dakota, meet my mother, Elizabeth."

"It's a pleasure to meet you, Mrs. Parker," I say warmly, extending my hand toward her. She gives me a quick but discerning look before accepting my hand and giving it a gentle pat.

"You certainly have that American charm," she remarks, turning back to Harry. "Well, come along, let's make our way to the lounge. I'm eager to catch up."

We follow Elizabeth down the hallway, Harry and I walking side by side. Taking our places on the couch, Harry settles in beside me, his arms casually draping over the backrest while his mother gracefully crosses her legs, adjusting her dress with an air of elegance.

"Where's Father?" Harry inquires, leaning back and resting his arms behind me on the couch.

"Oh, you know him. Always immersed in some late-night case," Elizabeth replies, her tone fills with familiarity.

"Oh, I forgot your dad is a cop," I unintentionally blurt out, momentarily contemplating whether I should pursue legal action against Logan.

"A detective, dear," Elizabeth corrects me. "Florence, dear, would you mind making us some tea?" A shy-looking girl appears momentarily before disappearing into the kitchen. Elizabeth turns her attention back to me, clearing her throat. "Harry mentioned your book, Dakota. I must say, I'm quite impressed."

"Why, thank you. Which one did he tell you about?" I inquire politely, mustering a smile.

"Oh, there's more than one?" Elizabeth responds, her surprise evident.

"Yes, Mother. The other one is exclusively published in America," Harry interjects.

"I see. And do you have other plans, especially now that you'll be joining Harry in China this time?" Elizabeth probes, her words lace with a hint of mystery.

"You mean for another book?" I seek clarification.

"No, no. I mean for other aspects of your life," she says, implying something deeper.

"Well, I currently work part-time for the Daily Shere, and I have no plans of quitting anytime soon," I reply, maintaining a pleasant smile.

"Oh? But—" Elizabeth's sentence is cut short as a car pulls into the driveway, momentarily flooding the room with its lights before vanishing. "That must be your father. Let me go attend to that," Elizabeth says, offering a sweet smile as she departs from the room.

"I'll walk with you, Mother," Harry volunteers, casting a *look* in my direction before they both leave the room. Left alone, Florence, the young girl who had been assisting us, brings our tea and gently sets it down on the table, her movements quiet and precise. She then quietly retreats back to the kitchen, leaving me in a momentary silence as the faint sound of footsteps fades away.

I sink into the couch, allowing myself a moment of solitude to gather my thoughts. My body feels burdened, weighed down by the racing thoughts that refuse to grant me rest. It becomes clear that this gathering, intended as a distraction, is unable to quell the turbulent storm that rages within me. The mention of going to China fades into insignificance amidst the overwhelming presence of Logan and the unanswered questions that haunt my mind.

In the stillness, my thoughts race in relentless pursuit, each one vying for attention, each one offering its own interpretation. Did Harry come back for a reason?

Was his silent treatment a calculated strategy, a form of punishment designed to make me reflect upon my actions? The whirlwind of uncertainty leaves me breathless, my mind struggling to grasp a sense of clarity amidst the chaos. The room around me fades into a hazy backdrop as I delve into the depths of my own thoughts; I clench my fists tightly, feeling the pressure building in my palms as my nails leave half-moon imprints on my skin. The sharp pain shoots through my fingers, a stark reminder of the tension that consumes me. In a desperate attempt to regain composure, I release my grip, allowing the tension to dissipate.

Soon enough, the sound of approaching footsteps breaks through the haze of my thoughts. I adjust my posture, assuming a more composed demeanor as Harry enters the room accompanied by his father, followed closely by Elizabeth.

"You must be Dakota. It's a pleasure to finally meet you," Mr. Parker greets me with a firm handshake, his demeanor serious and composed. With that, he proceeds toward the dining table, accompanied by Elizabeth and Harry.

Taking my seat beside Harry, I find myself amidst a lively discussion between the men, their topics flowing in a torrent. Elizabeth interjects with occasional remarks, and I strive to maintain an appearance of engagement, nodding and offering polite smiles throughout the meal. The aromas of the food fill the air, mingling with their pleasant chatter. In the midst of this familial gathering, Florence is joined by another lady who gracefully presents the tea and dishes to the table. As the men share laughter over an anecdote I seemed to have missed, Elizabeth's voice breaks through the cheerful ambiance.

"Oh, that reminds me," she interjects, capturing the attention of everyone at the table, including me. "Dakota, Harry told us about the little incident that happened."

My brows furrow in confusion, the sudden mention of an incident catching me off guard.

"Incident? What incident?" I inquire, my curiosity piques. Harry offers me a sympathetic gaze, his hand gently rubbing my back as I search for understanding.

"It was difficult for me to come home and see her in that state," he reveals, his voice carrying a weight of emotion. The room falls silent for a moment as the gravity of his words settles upon them.

Ah, that incident.

"I could only imagine how traumatic that must have been," Elizabeth reaches out to hold Harry's hand, her concern evident in her touch. "What were you thinking, going to such a dangerous place alone at night?" Elizabeth's accusatory tone pierces the air, her words laden with a mixture of worry and reproach.

"I wasn't alone," I reply coolly, my voice carrying a hint of defiance. "I was with my best friend."

"So, two girls alone at night in a bar?" Elizabeth retorts, her skepticism coloring her words.

"No, we weren't alone—" I pause, letting out a weary sigh, feeling the onset of a headache adding to the turmoil inside my mind. "It didn't even happen at the bar; it happened today." I turn my gaze toward Harry, disbelief etches on my face.

When did he even have the chance to divulge this information to them?

"She's right, mother. But it could have been prevented if she hadn't gone to that bar," Harry interjects, his hand finding its way to my leg, gripping it gently, silently urging me to hold my tongue.

"Regardless, none of this would have happened if she hadn't gone," Elizabeth concludes firmly, her statement resonating with a tone of finality. "London bars are just pits of sin."

"I believe she has learned her lesson, Mother," Harry interjects matter-of-factly, his grip on my leg tightening slightly as a silent reminder for me to shut up.

"It's good to hear that. A bar is no place for a lady," Mr. Parker adds, leaning forward in his chair, his stern gaze fixed upon me, his words carrying a weight of traditional values.

In the midst of their judgments and assumptions, I feel that same nasty storm brewing inside me yet again. But for the moment, I choose to bite my tongue, allowing their words to wash over me, even as a sense of dissatisfaction settles deep within my heart.

As the conversation about *the incident* carries on, I find myself sinking deeper into the chair, a wave of annoyance and defeat washing over me. My gaze shifts down to Harry's hand resting on my leg, a subtle gesture that feels suffocating at this moment. Every fiber of my being yearns to push it away, to escape from this place and run, just like Forrest Gump, with no intention of stopping.

I divert my attention to my own hands, lifting them slightly and examining the swollen fingers that resemble little sausages. At that moment, Noah's smiling face flashes in my mind, his unwavering support and understanding becoming a lifeline in this sea of judgment. I wonder what he would have said or done if he were here, providing me with the security and comfort that feels so distant amidst the critical gazes of the judgmental police officer and Harry's holier-than-thou mother.

The thought of Noah's presence offers a fleeting sense of solace, but I quickly realize that security is a luxury I won't find in this setting. The weight of judgment and the noticeable tension in the room remind me that I'm alone in navigating this nasty storm, left to confront the consequences of my actions without a lifeline to lean on.

After a tumultuous night, one that left me feeling miserable, we bid farewell to Harry's parents. As Harry closes my car door and settles into the driver's seat, his fingers fumble with the seatbelt.

The anger still courses through my veins, and I can no longer contain it.

"Did you really have to tell your parents?" I question, surprising myself with the calmness in my voice despite the raging emotions within me.

"Dakota, my father is a detective. It's important to have him on our side in this situation. I did it to protect you," Harry explains, his voice fill with determination.

I remain silent, and Harry reaches out to tenderly stroke my cheek, guiding my gaze toward him. "Listen, you know I only want what's best for you, right? Dakota, I would do anything to prevent something like this from happening again. The mere thought of what could have happened if I hadn't been there today is unbearable," Harry confesses, his breaths uneven with the weight of the moment. He starts the engine, a gentle hum filling the car.

The overwhelming cocktail of guilt, anger, and sadness becomes too heavy to bear, and all I desire is to retreat to the solace of my home. Perhaps there, in the quiet solitude, I can allow myself to break down and confront the storm of emotions that rages within me.

Alone.

"Harry, could you please take me home?" I manage to utter, my voice betraying the cracks in my composure.

"We are going home, my love," Harry responds, a gentle smile adorning his face, his hand instinctively reaching for my leg.

"No, I mean to my own house," I assert firmly, delicately

removing his hand from my leg, avoiding the dreadful squeeze that usually follows.

Harry's expression shifts, concern etching across his face as he studies mine. I stare out the window, my gaze fixes on the passing scenery.

"Dakota, my house is closer," he says, attempting to persuade me.

"Harry, I just need to sleep in my own bed," I assert, my voice pleading for understanding.

"Alone?" Harry's voice turns cold, his eyes fixes on the road ahead.

"Yes… please," I respond, the tears threatening to spill over but held back through sheer determination.

Silence hangs heavy between us, and though Harry doesn't utter a word, I can sense his disappointment as he accelerates, propelling us towards my house.

11

The comforting embrace of my own bed works wonders on my overwhelmed soul, providing a much-needed time-out. With each splash of water in the shower, the lingering scent of Elizabeth's overpowering perfume, which had clung to my hair like an unwelcome presence, dissipate, allowing me to breathe freely once again. Last night's events had undoubtedly left a less-than-ideal first impression, and if I never crossed paths with Harry's parents again, it would likely be too soon. And I'm certain that the feeling is mutual; perhaps distance is the best solution for all parties involved.

With my damp hair clinging to my shoulders, I navigate my way to the kitchen, relishing in the tranquility of my own company. However, the tranquility is abruptly shattered by a knock on the door, disrupting the fragile peace that had settled within me. Curiosity ting with caution, I approach the door and peer through the peephole, revealing Harry's familiar face adorned with a broad grin. In his hands, he holds a carefully arranged bouquet of vibrant crimson roses.

"I'm taking you out today," he declares with enthusiasm as I open the door. Planting a gentle peck on my cheek, he presents the flowers as a token of his affection.

"Harry, no," I interject, gently moving the flowers aside to meet his gaze. "I really need to talk to you."

The joy that was once painted across his face fades, replaced by a sense of concern as he detects the seriousness in my voice.

"We're going to Hyde Park; we can talk there, okay?" Harry suggests, lightly pinching my cheeks in an attempt to lighten the mood. I instinctively pull back, shaking my head in response. Sensing my hesitation, he lets out a sigh, placing his hands on my shoulders; he speaks with a mix of desperation and exasperation.

"Jesus, Dakota, not this again."

After a moment of contemplation, I almost give in to his request. But then, a wave of determination washes over me. I am well aware of how the day will unfold; our conversations will not delve into matters of significance. Instead, he will flood me with an overwhelming array of gifts, treats, and various forms of entertainment at this park, all designed to divert attention away from engaging in this conversation I have been requesting.

It's time for this cycle of uncertainty to end.

Stepping away from Harry, I turn to place the roses on my kitchen counter. I'm tired of always giving in, tired of not being able to assert myself. I take a deep breath to gather my courage. Turning back to face Harry, I meet his shock expression head-on.

"No," I finally say, my voice fill with resolve. "We can talk here."

After a few seconds of heavy silence, Harry shakes his head, his gaze directs downward. The atmosphere in the room becomes tense as we stand there, both grappling with our emotions.

"What has gotten into you, Dakota? When did you become so difficult?" he exclaims, his frustration evident in his tone.

"I'm not being difficult just for saying no—" I begin to explain, but Harry interrupts, throwing his hands up in defeat.

"You know what," he interjects, his voice lace with annoyance, "I came here to do something nice for you, especially after yesterday. If your only plan is to start a fight, I'd rather just go by myself."

"I'm trying to have a conversation with you, not a fight," I retort, feeling the frustration rise within me.

"Dakota, I had a long day, and I'm not in the mood for this," Harry says, his voice strained. "Either you come with me to the park, or I go alone." His gaze pierces through me, waiting for my response. I scoff and look away, knowing that nothing I say will be truly heard.

Harry takes my silence as his answer and storms toward the door, the weight of our unspoken words hanging heavy in the air. The sound of the door slamming shut reverberates through the room, intensifying the tension that remains.

Feeling the weight of it all, I release a heavy sigh, my shoulders slumping under the burden.

After about five minutes, the sound of another knock echoes through my quiet house. I find myself standing in the same spot, torn between the desire to ignore it and the curiosity that nags at the back of my mind. Another, more impatient knock echoes through the house, urging me to make a decision.

With anger pulsing through my veins, I march toward the door, my footsteps resonating with determination. Each step fuels my resolve, and by the time I reach the door, my emotions are ready to spill forth. I'm prepared to unleash a torrent of words to let Harry know exactly what I think of his thoughtless actions.

As the door swings open, my heart skips a beat, but the sight that greets me is far from what I expected. In an instant, a hand shoots out, wrapping around my throat with a fierce grip, forcefully propelling me backward into my own home. Logan's eyes bloodshot and filled with rage, boring into mine with a chilling intensity. Gasping for air, I find myself suspended against the wall, my feet dangling helplessly in the air. Panic surges through me as I fight to draw in a precious breath, my body desperate for oxygen. Frantically, I attempt to pry his vice-like grip from around my neck, my hands clawing at his fingers in a desperate bid for release.

But in a sudden twist, his grip weakens, and I crumple to the ground, desperately gulping for air. He stands there, visibly shaken, running a trembling hand through his disheveled hair. His gaze becomes distant, lost in some unseen abyss.

"You," he mutters, his eyes darting to meet mine, his voice laces with venom, "you... fucking slut!" His words strike like thunder rumbles through the air, leaving me stunned and vulnerable.

A gasp escapes my lips, my heart sinking to the depths of the devil himself as I raise my gaze to meet his.

"Here I was, feeling so damn guilty after you ran away from me. I actually thought you had some genuine feelings for that guy from the bar, that it wasn't just some random hookup in the parking lot. But now, I find you here, cozying up with a whole different guy," he sneers, his laughter devoid of any humor.

I steady my breathing, my hands tenderly caressing my throbbing throat, while his gaze fixates on the bouquet of roses sitting on my kitchen counter. He picks them up, inhaling their fragrance, a dark smile playing on his lips. In an instant, he raises the vase high above his head.

"No—" I begin, my voice desperate, but it falls on deaf ears. The glass shatters with a resounding crash, droplets of water, and fragments of glass raining down around me. The roses tumble to the floor, forgotten. I instinctively retreat, my legs scrambling me away from the dangerous shards now littering my sanctuary. He nonchalantly kicks aside a few pieces as he slowly advances towards me, a malevolent gleam in his eyes.

"You girls are all the same," he hisses, the venom dripping from his words, and my heart pounds in my chest, fear pulsating through my veins. The familiar sensation of dread envelops me, and I silently remind myself to remain calm if I want to escape this encounter. Yet, a sense of impending danger lingers, and I struggle to shake off the suffocating tension.

The room falls into a brutal silence, the absence of sound

amplifying the weight of the atmosphere. Every breath feels too loud, and I find myself holding mine as if to avoid drawing any attention. At that moment, our gazes collide, his eyes piercing into mine with an intensity that sends shivers down my spine. "It's a good thing you're so damn beautiful," he utters, his words carrying an unsettling mix of possessiveness and menace. The compliment hangs in the air like a sickly sweet poison, a stark contrast to the dangerous undertones of his demeanor.

In one swift, aggressive motion, he seizes my throat once again, forcibly pressing me against the unyielding wall. The impact sends shockwaves of pain vibrating through my body, and I struggle to catch my breath under his suffocating grip. His piercing gaze locks onto mine, a sinister mix of possessiveness and desire etches across his face. His thumb traces a chilling path along my chin, his touch an unsettling contrast to the violence of his actions.

"So beautiful," he whispers, his words dripping with a twisting fascination, his lips dangerously close to mine. My heart races, a mixture of fear and revulsion intertwining within me. But then, as abruptly as he seized me, his focus shifts, his eyes darting away, and he releases his grip once again. Confusion clouds my thoughts as he speaks, his tone fills with a mocking sneer.

"I must admit, Dakota, I can see why you're so infatuated with these guys. Jesus, they're really good-looking dudes. You seem to have a type. Tall, dark hair, and that polished business look." He whistles before he leans in, our noses almost touching, his gaze unwavering and menacing. "Does my blonde hair not arouse you? Perhaps I can persuade you to change your mind."

His words hang in the air like a vile taunt, and I recoil; every instinct in me urges me to escape, to break free from this twisted entanglement.

My heart lurches with a mix of fear and disgust as his lips forcefully collide with mine, his tongue aggressively invading my mouth. I instinctively resist, turning my head to the side, desperately gasping for precious air.

"Stop," I manage to whisper, my plea muffled by the unwelcome intrusion. Finally, he releases me, his eyes boring into mine with an unsettling intensity, his thumb tracing my cheek as he smirks.

The smile that curves his lips sends shivers down my spine, a chilling manifestation of his distorted desires.

"Tell me something, Dakota," he says, his tone lace with a disturbing mix of curiosity and frustration. "I'm trying to comprehend this. To understand you, women, you always spout these things about wanting a nice guy, someone genuine, honest, and straightforward. Yet, it seems the assholes always win in the end. Is that why you ran away? Am I not the bad boy you crave?"

I shake my head, unable to formulate a coherent response amid the chaos of my emotions. In a sudden burst of anger, he slams his hand against the wall, causing me to flinch instinctively. He leans in closer, his intense gaze penetrating my soul. "Answer me," he hisses, his breath hot against my skin.

My heart pounds so hard that I can barely think. I try to come up with a convincing lie, but I know he won't believe me. I blink back tears, desperately trying to avoid his gaze.

"I'm sorry," I whisper.

He scoffs, his dissatisfaction palpable, intensifying the impending dread within me. Preparing myself for the worst, bracing against the unknown terrors he might unleash, I barely have time to steady myself before Logan seizes me, his forceful kiss propelling my head against the wall.

Resistance becomes my sole instinct, futilely attempting to repel his advances. His grip constricts around my waist, fingers digging mercilessly into my flesh. Desperation fuels my every movement as I kick and wriggle, yearning for liberation from his grasp. A sudden, sharp agony jolts through my lower lip, his biting assault like a wannabe vampire sinking his teeth into me.

Summoning the remnants of my strength, I deliver a resolute kick, causing him to stagger backward. Blood trickles from my wounded lip; in an act of sheer determination, I again channel my remaining fortitude into a forceful punch, striking his face with all my might. His head jerks to the side, momentarily disoriented. However, my escape is foiled as he seizes me by the hair, cruelly dragging me to the ground. As I meet the ground once more, he paces restlessly, muttering to himself while I strive to maintain focus, inhaling deep breaths to anchor my trembling composure.

Every fiber of my being cries out for escape, the urgency surging through my veins. I must find a way out, away from this dangerous situation that threatens my safety and sanity.

I will my trembling limbs to rise, and with determination, I propel myself forward, sprinting toward the fireplace, where a stand of pokers awaits. Each step echoes with the throbbing ache in my hand, a poignant reminder of the forceful punch I had landed on him mere moments ago. Clenching my fist tightly around the cold, unyielding steel, I arm myself, bracing for the imminent confrontation. He approaches me deliberately, a sinister slowness in his gait. The gravity of the situation intensifies as he breaks the silence with a disconcerting remark, shattering any remnants of normalcy.

"Oh, this is awkward. I probably should've mentioned that I have a gun." The words hang in the air, thick with a foreboding unease.

As the surge of adrenaline courses through my veins once more, it fuels me to protect myself regardless. With urgency lacing my plea, I implore,

"Please, think about what you're doing."

In response, he unleashes a racket of deranged laughter, his sanity unraveling before my eyes.

"What am I doing? Oh, how wrong you are, Dakota. It's

what you did," he retorts, drawing closer with a menacing snarl, accusatory finger pointing in my direction. "This is all your fault."

With a sinister smile, he reveals the gun, its significance laden with a disturbing aura. He scratches the back of his head with its muzzle, a chilling display of his deranged state. "What I am doing," he repeats, punctuating his words with another derisive laugh. "I saw you fuck one man in his car after we met. And then, today, I saw a completely different man leaving your house. Yet, I need to think about my actions?"

Suddenly, I find myself sprawled on the ground, clutching my throbbing face, while Logan's gaze pierces through me with a venomous intensity. My eyes drift downward, drawn to my trembling hand, witnessing the crimson hues of my own blood shimmering under the gentle sunlight that seeps through the windows. As realization dawns upon him, Logan's eyes widen, mirroring my own disbelief at the injury I now bear, causing him to slowly lower the gun once again.

His frustration erupts into an explosive yell, shattering the tense atmosphere. However, I gather every ounce of resilience to intervene, struggling to regain my footing. With a fierce determination, I remind myself to remain composed and take measured breaths, desperately attempting to bring forth reason amidst the chaos.

"Please," I implore, my words stumbling out in a desperate plea, my voice quivering with the weight of my explanation. I search desperately for any glimmer of reason in his eyes, a sign that he might listen, that he might understand.

But I don't even understand.

In response, he smirks devilishly, his words dripping with a sinister allure.

"Ah, Dakota, the begging. It's so hot," he remarks, licking his lips in a manner that sends chills down my spine.

"Logan," I plead once again, my voice tings with defeat and the searing pain that courses through me after the brutal impact of the gun. "Please."

He mocks my plea, his voice filled with taunting indifference. "Please? Please, what, Dakota?" he echoes, nonchalantly shrugging. "Please, you? Well, that could certainly be arranged." He licks his lips once more, his wicked smile deepening, reveling in the power he holds over me. "Consummating our relationship, what a brilliant idea, Dakota."

Disbelief washes over me, rendering me speechless for a moment. I instinctively recoil, stepping back until the unyielding fireplace obstructs my retreat. Desperation fills my eyes as I raise the poker once again, its presence serving as my feeble shield, determine to protect myself. Yet, Logan reaches out, his hands reaching for mine, attempting to disarm me.

Summoning every ounce of willpower, I swing the poker with all my might, connecting with his arm. A paining wince escapes his lips, momentarily halting his advance as I seize the opportunity to bolt toward the door.

However, he swiftly catches up to me, pressing my head forcefully against the door, his grip on my wrists tightening with a bone-crushing intensity. The poker slips from my grasp, clattering to the ground, an emblem of my fleeting defense.

His arms ensnare my waist, yanking me mercilessly closer to him. In a whirlwind motion, he spins me around, his grip solid as he lifts me effortlessly before releasing me onto the hard ground. The impact jolts through my body, searing pain reverberating through every nerve. A scream escapes my lips, echoing the agony that courses through me. Yet, his lips forcefully meet mine once more, effectively muffling my cries as I desperately kick and punch, fighting for my freedom.

His intentions become clear as he attempts to strip away my clothing, a violation I refuse to endure. Squirming and writhing,

I strive to evade his grasp, determine to retain my dignity. Frustrated by my resistance, he delivers a brutal punch to my face, the resounding impact ringing in my ears, temporarily drowning out his insidious kisses. My eyes flutter open and shut, blurred vision struggling to focus; I catch a glimpse of the gun lying nearby, a potential lifeline.

Summoning the last bit of strength in me, I extend my trembling fingers, reaching out for the gun as his attention remains fixated on undressing me. Oblivious to my intentions, he tightens his grip on my jeans, consumed by his depraved desires. Seizing the opportunity, I silently employ my fingers to draw the gun closer, my grip tightening around its weight. Pressing it against his temple, I hold my breath, steeling myself for what comes next.

A sinister grin stretches across his face, his voice laced with arrogance.

"You won't do it, Dakota," he taunts, underestimating the depth of my desperation.

"Get the fuck off of me," I demand, forcefully pushing him away with the muzzle. He sits on his knees, hands raised. I stand up, unsteady on my feet, and wipe my hair out of my face. With hate in my eyes, I extend the gun toward him, holding it tightly as I take several cautious steps backward.

"Put the gun down, Dakota, before you hurt yourself," he warns, his voice tings with a mix of concern and caution.

"Stop talking! Just stop fucking talking!" I scream, my grip tightening on the gun, both hands clasping it tightly. Logan raises his hands further, a futile attempt to pacify me, but I sense his impending movement.

"No, stay down there," I bark, my heart pounding within my chest, the rush of adrenaline coursing through my veins.

"Okay, okay, Dakota. Just calm down," he pleads, desperately attempting to reason with my erratic behavior.

But how could I possibly calm down? My tears mingle with the blood staining my face, my fists trembling as I clutch the gun with white-knuckled determination.

"Calm down? Are you fucking kidding me? Look at what you have done to me," I sob, my voice foreign to my own ears. "You have done nothing but hurt me, Logan, while I took the blame for everything."

"I'm sorry," Logan's voice quavers as he rises to his feet, his hands still held up in surrender.

My narrow eyes betray a smoldering anger, and I apply even more pressure to the trigger.

"Just put the gun down, and let's talk," he pleads, his voice lace with desperation.

"I'm done talking, Logan. With you. With Harry, I'm fucking done," I sneer, bitterness dripping from my words like poison. "Stay down, Logan."

He takes a step toward me, but I raise the gun without flinching, a steely resolve burning within me.

"Dakota, please," he begs, his voice cracking with fear and regret.

Without a second thought, I pull the trigger, unleashing the devastating impact. Logan crumples to the ground, writhing in agonizing pain. My heart pounding fiercely within my chest, with shaking hands, I fumble for my phone, retrieving it from my bag, my fingers trembling as I dial 999, seeking the help that I desperately need in this harrowing moment.

In the midst of Logan's anguish, cries reverberating through the air, the distant wailing of sirens intensifying, and the vivid red and blue lights flooding into my living room, the overwhelming sense of gravity descends upon me; the weight of what just unfolded settles squarely on my weary shoulders. The gun slips from my trembling hand, and I find myself sinking to my knees, a torrent of emotions surging within me. As the ensuing commotion engulfs the scene, Logan is apprehended and led away. A compassionate police officer approaches me, his empathetic smile offering solace in the midst of chaos.

"Dakota," he says, his voice brimming with understanding, "I'll accompany you to the hospital for a thorough check-up before recording your statement. Is that okay with you?"

His gentle tone providing a glimmer of comfort amidst the storm. I nod in silent agreement, a wave of relief washing over me as I realize that this arduous ordeal is finally over. It is time for me to bid farewell to the chaos that Logan has woven into the fabric of my life, embracing a future free from his destructive influence.

Hopefully.

12

Before the bathroom mirror of the hospital, I stand, confronted by a visage of anguish and pain. My once-unblemished face now bears the cruel marks of a violent encounter—bruises painted in hues of black and blue, a split lip, and a swollen cheek. With a heavy heart, I gather the strength to lift my shirt, exposing a canvas of finger-shaped bruises adorning my vulnerable stomach. As tears brim in my eyes, I find myself transfixed by the reflection staring back at me, struggling to comprehend the starkness of the reality before my very eyes. The radiant joy that once illuminated my gaze has faded into a distant memory, replaced by a solemn emptiness as I confront the image of a stranger who stares back at me.

The passage of time seems like an eternity, and I realize that I have not slept, eaten, or even returned to the failed sanctuary of my home. This day has been an unrelenting barrage of medical examinations, recounting the horror I endured, enduring scans, and facing an onslaught of interviews. Fatigue gnaws at my bones, and weariness seeps into my very being.

All I yearn for now is the solace of home, a place free from the terror that haunts me. Yet, even the mere thought of returning there sends shivers down my spine. Desperation claws at my soul, urging me to escape this sterile confinement and find refuge anywhere but here.

Run, Forrest, run.

A gentle tap on the bathroom door rouses me from the depths of my ruminations. With a touch of compassion, a police officer steps into the room, extending my phone towards me.

"I thought you might want this," she murmurs, her voice carrying the weight of understanding. Accepting the device, I offer a fragile smile, grateful for this small act of kindness. As she retreats, I find myself transfixed by the screen, its glow illuminating my troubled face. With a swift motion, I unlock the phone, my trembling fingers embarking on a quest to find solace in Noah's name within my messages.

Only to be met with confusion. A sense of bewilderment engulfs me as I close and reopen the messenger app, desperately seeking his presence, but to no avail.

Then, like a bolt of lightning, realization strikes. In a moment of clarity, I navigate to my blocked numbers, and there, in poignant isolation, lies Noah's name. Disappointment wells within me, a testament to the choice Harry made in haste. With a sigh, I release him from his digital exile, my fingertip hovering over the call button, poise between hesitation and longing.

"Where is she?" The resounding bellow reverberates through the hallway, shattering my focus on Noah's number illuminating on my phone screen. I pivot toward the door, my heart seizing with anticipation, as Harry forcefully bursts into the hospital room. His piercing gaze sweeps over my battered form, painstakingly cataloging the bruises and lacerations that paint my face and body, a testament to the pain I have endured. An anguished contortion dances across his features, merging disbelief and anger into a tumultuous mixture, leaving me suspended in a fragile limbo, awaiting his reaction.

After an interminable stretch of tense silence, he finally finds his voice. "Jesus..." The word escapes his lips in a breathless exhale, laden with the weight of his inability to articulate his thoughts. I anticipate further words, a cascade of emotions to fill the void, but instead, I witness the visible struggle etched upon his face. It becomes apparent that he grapples with the daunting task of comprehending the profound sight before him.

Seeking refuge from his scrutinizing gaze, I stride purposefully toward the hospital bed, deliberately taking a seat, determine to shield myself from the intensity of his presence. Despite my efforts to detach, I can't help but confront him with a tone devoid of emotion.

"Are you just going to stand there, staring?" My words are a stark reminder of his prolonged silence. Harry shakes his head, his admission punctuated by a slight, defeated gesture.

"I don't know what to say," he confesses, his vulnerability evident. My eyebrow arches involuntarily, startled by his uncharacteristic inability to find words at this moment.

"Where?" he presses, his unwavering gaze still searing into the depths of my being.

"Where, what, Harry?" I sigh, the weight of exhaustion etching lines of weariness upon my forehead, instantly triggering a throbbing headache.

"Where did he take you?" he demands, his voice escalating in volume, each word lace with urgency.

"Nowhere," I reply, my fingers absently twirling the threadbare hospital blanket, the gesture offering a feeble distraction from the mounting tension. Harry's eyes shut tightly, his jaw clenched in a futile attempt to contain the maelstrom of emotions raging within him. Inhaling deeply, he opens his eyes once more, fixing his gaze upon me.

"What do you mean nowhere? You were at your house the whole time?" he exclaims, a mix of incredulity and frustration seeping into his voice. My nod further shatters his resolve, causing his countenance to crumble in disappointment.

"I was right there," he continues, his tone tings with despondency. Harry averts his gaze, his hand rubbing his forehead, as the weight of defeat and anger intertwine upon his face. "Dakota, you should have screamed. You should have tried—" His words slice through the air, but I halt him before he can delve deeper into the realm of what-ifs.

"Stop, just stop talking," I interject, my voice hushes but infused with a raw intensity that belies the numbing pain that engulfs me.

Harry moves to the bed and wraps his arms around me, pulling me close to him and holding my face close to his chest.

"I wish you never went to that bar," he whispers, his hand tracing soothing patterns along my back.

Yet, the numbness that once cloaked my emotions begins to yield, making way for a fiery surge of anger that surges from deep within my chest, coursing toward my flushed visage. Swiftly extricating myself from Harry's grasp, I leave him bewilder by my sudden withdrawal.

"You can't be serious," I assert, my voice ting with a mixture of incredulity and frustration.

"What?" His genuine perplexity colors his response, his confusion palpable.

"You can't just be here for me without blaming me?" I demand, my tone carrying a resolute edge.

"I am here," he sighs, frustration etched in his voice. "Damn it, why didn't you just come with me?"

"Please, stop talking," I interject, my voice steady but lace with a plea for silence, for respite.

"If you never went—" Harry starts again, but I cut him off, my words brimming with a sense of determination.

"You can leave," I declare, feeling as though I am taking a leap off a cliff, a leap that is mine alone to take. "I want you to leave."

Harry's mouth hangs open momentarily, a semblance of words hovering on his lips, only to be swallowed back into the depths of his silence. His eyes fixate forward, grappling to comprehend the weight of my words. I can sense his struggle, his mind striving to process the magnitude of what I have just expressed.

"You need me," he finally speaks up, his voice tinged with an undercurrent of desperation. "Especially now."

"No," I assert, my voice resolute and unwavering. "I *need* you to leave," I reiterate, punctuating my words with conviction. I offer a humorless laugh laced with a bitter realization. "And not just this room."

He rises from his seat, his eyes closing momentarily as his fingers run through his disheveled hair.

"Dakota, please don't do this," he implores, his voice carrying a mix of pleading and disbelief. "We can get through this. You're just emotional and tired, thinking irrationally."

"You're right, Harry. I am tired," I concede, my voice heavy with the weight of accumulating frustration. "Tired of the constant inability to have a normal conversation with you, free from interruptions and unfounded blame. I am exhausted from the invasion of my privacy, with you checking my phone and blocking numbers. Yes, I went to a fucking bar. So what? Given the chance, I would make the same choice all over again."

Rising from the bed, I fix him with a piercing gaze, bitterness etch in every line of my face. "You left, Harry. You fucking left without so much as a text. And now, suddenly, you reappear without any remorse or apology? As if you didn't let me walk away in the middle of the night? As if you didn't vanish from my life for weeks, leaving me to grapple with your absence? You left, and now I'm telling you to do it again."

His gaze meets mine, a potent blend of sadness and

desperation swirling within his eyes. With aching tenderness, he steps closer, gingerly clasping my hand with his own. His eyes scour mine, yearning for a glimmer of hope, only to be met with weariness and anguish. Drawing nearer, he caresses my cheek, his searching gaze swinging between the depths of my eyes as if seeking solace or guidance. Cupping my chin, he gently lifts my face, and his lips find mine in a kiss that, instead of igniting joy and passion, carries an undertone of farewell.

"I love you, Dakota. We will get through this," he whispers against my lips, his voice lace with a fervent plea.

A heavy sigh escapes my lips as another kiss lands upon them. I reluctantly withdraw, taking a step back, creating a tangible space between us.

"Dakota, I love you. I came back for you," he implores, sinking to his knees, his grip still firmly holding my hands. "I will be better. Just tell me what I can do."

I close my eyes, gently disentangling myself from his touch. His expression morphs into a frown, perplexed by my withdrawal. "What can I do?" he inquires, his voice tings with genuine concern.

"You can leave," I assert, my tone resolute and unwavering.

With a final, beseeching gaze, he rises to his feet and solemnly makes his way toward the door, his shoulders slump in a profound sense of defeat. As the latch clicks shut, I exhale a long, cathartic breath, sensing a tangible release as a weight lifts from my chest. Weary and emotionally spent, I lower myself onto the bed, succumbing to the exhaustion and overwhelming emotions that have consumed me throughout this uphill journey.

I retrieve my phone from my pocket and embark on a search for new towns nearby, seeking a destination that strikes a balance between being sufficiently distant and yet not too far if such a notion exists. After careful consideration, I fixate upon a place called Rye, and a surge of anticipation dances within my chest as

I peruse captivating images capturing the essence of this quaint little town. Motivated by a renewed sense of purpose, I navigate to my email and commence composing my resignation letter addressed to the Daily Shere, a profound sense of finality settling upon me with each keystroke. Contemplating whether to reach out to Noah, I wrestle with the fear of burdening him further with my emotional baggage, ultimately deciding to lock my phone and dismissing the notion of initiating the call.

13

As I pack the last few boxes into my car, I can't help but take one last glance at the now-empty home that I had created for myself. Closing the door, I take a deep breath before getting into the driver's seat. As the car engine purrs to life, I steal a glance at the rearview mirror, taking a moment to adjust my hat atop my head—a feeble yet instinctive attempt to conceal my bruised face from prying eyes. With determination coursing through my veins, I set forth on my journey, guiding the steering wheel toward the welcoming embrace of a nearby coffee shop, where I'll take a much-needed break before the hour-and-a-half trip to Rye.

As I patiently wait for my coffee, my eyes are magnetically drawn to Noah's name on my still-cracked phone screen. He remains the sole person I yearn to talk with, yet the mere thought of bidding him farewell amplifies the ache in my heart. The weight of saying goodbye is a burden I cannot bear at the moment. The truth is, I know I must first untangle the mess within me, confront the relentless PTSD inflicted upon me by Logan, and rediscover my own version of normalcy before intertwining another person into the chaos. I find myself pondering, beyond the comforting security I currently crave, what exactly do I desire from Noah?

Could it be a romantic relationship?

The idea lingers in my mind, but the timing feels utterly unfavorable. Noah has always been a constant source of solace in my life, unwavering in his support, and I cannot help but berate myself for not reaching out to him through a simple text message sooner. Regret fills me as I acknowledge that opening the door for Harry was a grave mistake. I should have stood my ground, said no earlier, firmly refusing to go with him from the start. If I had chosen to drive directly home after dropping Zoe off, I could have reached out to Noah and honestly conveyed my emotions, expressing how I truly felt.

Perhaps then, I would not find myself in this battered and bruised state.

However, dwelling on the 'what ifs' and 'should haves' serves no purpose now. The reflection on my phone screen reveals that while my bruises have somewhat faded, the chaos inside me still remains. I am a shattered mess, and it is imperative that I pick up the pieces before anything else. When I reach Rye, I will summon the courage to call Noah and unveil the entirety of my circumstances.

Yes, that's precisely what I will do.

I thank the barista as my coffee is ready and exit the coffee shop, placing the cup on the roof of my car. I dig through my bag, searching for my keys; my mind is filled with thoughts about the uncertain future. I know it is time to move on, to leave behind everything that had become too heavy to carry. It isn't easy to let go of the one person I long to hold onto, but I know it is necessary for my own well-being and his. I need time to heal and rediscover who I am. And I need to do it on my own, away from the toxicity that had consumed me for far too long. Moreover, I must acknowledge the sheer selfishness of my own desires, presuming that Noah would effortlessly comprehend and wholeheartedly embrace this situation.

"Dakota?" A voice calls out, causing me to swiftly pivot around, only to discover Noah's figure standing there. Caught off guard by his sudden presence, my heart skips a beat, a rush of emotions surging within me. Even in this unexpected encounter, Noah's captivating beauty remains undiminished, an ethereal sight that leaves me breathless. With a deliberate motion, he raises his fingers toward the brim of my hat, tenderly lifting it away from my face. As the fabric retreats, I draw in a quivering breath, surrendering to the vulnerability that blossoms in the space between us. His unwavering gaze, sharp and penetrating, traverses the landscape of my features, swiftly honing in on the lingering marks of bruises and injuries that still taint my skin.

"You're leaving?" he softly queries, his eyes brimming with a potent mix of emotions, seeking solace and clarity within the depths of my own. The lump in my throat swells, hindering my ability to respond with ease as I grapple with the weight of our impending separation.

"Yes," I manage to utter, my voice carrying the weight of inevitability. With my gaze shifting intermittently between Noah and the car awaiting my departure, I find myself ill-prepared for the intensity of this encounter. Confronting him at this moment becomes an arduous task, a surge of conflicting emotions threatening to overwhelm me.

A wistful sigh escapes my lips, the longing for an easier path echoing within me. "A phone call would have been so much simpler," I whisper, acknowledging the undeniable truth that a conversation from a distance would have spared us the anguish of this face-to-face farewell.

"Noah," I murmur, my gaze momentarily dropping before lifting it back to meet his, a silent resolve to hold back the tears welling within me. "I'm sorry for not reaching out to you," I confess, my voice carrying the weight of regret. As my eyes shimmer with unshed tears, I desperately need him to hear the truth, to grasp that my silence was never a deliberate act of shutting him out.

A heavy sigh escapes my lips, my vulnerability laid bare. "Harry, unexpectedly showed up, and before I could even fathom the situation, he had already blocked your number. I would never purposefully ignore you, but by the time I realized what had happened, it felt like it was too late to rectify."

Noah nods, his eyes brimming with understanding rather than harboring any hint of anger or annoyance.

"Dakota, I've heard about what happened," he sighs, a visible display of frustration at the unfortunate circumstances. "I'm so sorry."

In that shared moment of empathy, I find comfort in knowing that Noah harbors no ill will toward me, only compassion and a genuine desire to comprehend the complexities of the situation at hand. Closing the distance between us, I move closer to him, acutely aware of the shimmering tears that glisten in his eyes. My expression softens as his unwavering gaze delicately follows the path of my injuries, his thumb tenderly brushing against the bruise on my cheek, leaving a trail of gentle solace in its wake.

His eyes betray his agony; his jaw clenched tightly in an effort to suppress the anguish within. The sight tugs at the strings of my heart, a desperate plea that beckons me to offer comfort in the form of an embrace. His gaze locks with mine once more, and in that moment, I can no longer resist the overwhelming urge.

Without hesitation, I envelop him in my arms, seeking to provide a sanctuary amidst the chaos. As he reciprocates the embrace, his touch brings comfort. Inhaling deeply, I relish the sensation as he nuzzles the crook of my neck, his presence a soothing balm to the wounds within; my lungs fill with a deep, fortifying breath, attempting to steady the tremors in my voice.

"Noah," I whisper, my voice trembling with a mixture of relief and vulnerability. "God, what a mess," I sigh, unable to contain the few tears that escape my eyes. "I've thought about reaching out to you countless times."

"Why didn't you?" he asks, his voice heavy with concern and curiosity.

"I didn't want to drag you into this stupid mess," I admit. "First Harry, and then Logan. It all happened too fast for me to try and regain control."

His hold on me tightens as my words reach his ears. We cling to each other for a few more seconds, unwilling to let go.

Eventually, we slowly release each other, and I brush away a stray tear with my fingers.

"For what it's worth, I wouldn't have minded the mess," Noah's lips curl into a gentle smile, his touch tenderly wiping away another stray tear that graces my cheek.

As the weight of guilt threatens to consume me, I muster the courage to address the night that still lingers in my mind.

"About that night, I'm so sorry if I pushed you into something…" I pause, my voice strain with the memories of my own actions, the knowledge that I was the one who initiated the intimacy.

With unwavering sincerity, Noah shakes his head, his eyes brimming with warmth and understanding.

"No, don't apologize. We were both willing participants."

A chuckle escapes my lips, intermingling with my tears. "Oh, I thought maybe you were just caught up in the moment or something."

He reassures me, his voice filled with conviction. "Not at all. I don't have any regrets."

A surge of relief washes over me, a smile blossoming upon my lips as I meet his gaze.

"Neither do I," I respond, the weight of apprehension lifting from my shoulders.

"Dakota, I understand that your past few days have been

filled with chaos, and it's crucial for you to take the time to heal and recuperate, both physically and mentally. I am more than willing to step back and give you the space you need," Noah expresses, drawing nearer to me. With a tender touch, he cradles my face in his hands, his voice fill with sincerity, "I just want you to know that you hold a special place in my heart, and I genuinely care about you."

A real smile graces my lips as Noah, and I find solace in a serene and harmonious silence, our eyes effortlessly conveying profound emotions. With a heartfelt expression, I open up to him, revealing the depth of my feelings,

"Noah, I care about you too. I mistakenly believed that the timing wasn't right for us at the bar, but now I realize I was wrong." Reflecting on the complexity of my own thoughts, I confess, "I do understand the importance of sorting out my own feelings before moving forward, and I don't expect you to wait for me. However, I must admit that the idea of having you in my life genuinely makes me happy. But I understand that asking for your patience is a selfish request," I confess, a tinge of guilt coloring my words.

"I must say, I happen to be quite the connoisseur of patience," he playfully retorts, his words lace with a mischievous charm that effortlessly draws a delightful chuckle from deep within me. His warm smile remains steadfast, and his unwavering gaze captures my attention. "Dakota, you never have to face anything alone. I will always be your unwavering support, your lifeline whenever you need me."

As I gaze at him, a deep breath fills my lungs, and the burden I've carried these past days eases ever so slightly. Tears well up in my eyes, but he's there, his gentle thumb catching them as he lovingly wipes them away.

Gratitude fills my voice as I say, choked with emotion, "Thank you," accompanied by a nod.

His hands remain on my face, and a warm smile graces his lips. His eyes search mine, seeking permission. I offer a nod, and his smile widens before our lips meet. Our tongues intertwine in a mesmerizing dance, his hands cradling my face as I pull him closer, yearning for him, creating an unbreakable bond.

A long-awaited respite washes over me, gently dissolving the layers of anxiety and restlessness that had plagued my soul.

In Noah's presence, a profound sense of tranquility takes root, enfolding me in its comforting embrace. His touch is tender, a soothing caress devoid of any hint of force or restraint.

Neither of us harbors the slightest inclination to break the tender connection we share. Instead, we allow the power of our kiss to become a conduit for unspoken emotions. In that lingering embrace, our lips become the vessel through which we express the depths of our desires and unspoken affections. These sentiments, carefully guarded for the right moment, will one day be released into the world in spoken words, when the stars align and the timing becomes perfect.

Until then, this kiss serves as our sanctuary, our shared refuge.

As our lips reluctantly part, he leans forward, gently resting his forehead against mine. I feel the warmth of his breath caress my skin, a tender reminder of our closeness.

"Can I ask you for a favor?" he whispers, his voice barely audible yet brimming with vulnerability. With my eyes closed, I immerse myself in the lingering sensations, savoring every precious second as he presses another slow and beautiful kiss upon my lips.

My heart flutters within my chest, anticipation building as I reply,

"Of course," my voice lace with eagerness and trust.

Softly, he breathes out, his warm gaze seeking mine, "Please promise to let me know when you're safe." His plea hangs in the air, laden with genuine concern and the depth of his affection.

I nod, my eyes opening to meet his unwavering gaze, assuring him, "I will," the words resonating with determination and the unbreakable bond between us.

In a moment of hesitation, he sighs deeply, his searching eyes locking with mine as if reluctant to let go. However, I reach out and grasp his hand, an urgent impulse compelling me to share something significant.

"Noah," I speak, my voice laden with trust and vulnerability, "I'm going to Rye. Perhaps you could come visit?"

Relief washes over his face, a weight lifts from his shoulders, and a smile of reassurance graces his lips. Without hesitation, he pulls me closer, his hand still enveloping mine, the other cupping my face with gentle affection. Our lips meet once more, sealing our unspoken agreement.

"I would love to," he murmurs between kisses, his words carrying the promise of future moments to be cherished.

As I gaze into the rearview mirror, the image of Noah slowly recedes into the distance, his hand still suspended in a farewell wave. The echoes of our shared moments intertwine with the fading scenery, leaving behind a trail of bittersweet memories that will eventually fade like bruises, vanishing into the passage of time.

A gentle buzz resonates from my phone, resting on the dashboard, catching my attention. With a quick glance, I catch sight of a message from Noah. Instantly, a comforting warmth envelops my heart, infusing it with a soothing embrace. Redirecting my focus back to the road, I carry that warmth with me, a whispered promise of connection amidst the journey ahead.

The future stretches before me, an expanse of unknown possibilities, its outcome shrouded in uncertainty. I cannot claim to possess the power of foresight, unable to discern what lies ahead.

Yet, amidst this vast landscape of unpredictability, a rare sense of tranquility settles in me, embracing the uncertainty with open arms. For the first time in a while, I find solace in the unknown, embracing the notion that not everything needs to be meticulously planned or perfectly orchestrated, that it is okay to not have all the answers in this very moment, I come to terms with the enigmatic nature of life. I embrace the beauty of the present, finding consolation in the realization that, sometimes, it's okay to surrender to the mysteries that unfold before me.

It's okay,

I'm okay.

The End